# ANMOL, THE HEIR APPARENT

# ANMOL, THE HEIR APPARENT

**Devi Raghuvanshi**

Anecdote

Anecdote
Publishing House
*For the love of quality reading!*

**Anecdote Publishing House**
E-35-A, E Block, Gali No. 2 Ganesh Nagar,
Pandav Nagar Complex Delhi-110092

Published by Anecdote Publishing House


First Edition 2023

ISBN 978-81-963155-1-1

MRP ₹ **295**


Book Promoted and Marketed by Champ Readers Pvt. Ltd.

Cover and Layout by Graphic Tailor
Printed by Thomson Press (India) Ltd, New Delhi

# Dedication

To my Parents who made me to read and write, even though they were just farmers. This book is also dedicated to the people who have already highlighted a sense of duty and Dharma in the past.

The author is not an authority on old Indian literature and religious epics, so any mistake or wrong interpretation may kindly be taken as the content of the story.

# Acknowledgements

I acknowledge and express my gratitude to my wife SUSHMA, for the input, spell check and all the inspiration and ideas, I conceived watching the degree of her patience.

My elder daughter PREETI deserves special thanks for the content resource, for the emotional and financial support in bringing out the publication of this book.

I would like PAYAL, my younger daughter to be a partner in this endeavour. Frankly speaking I have copied some of her blogs to make my book rich and true.

I would also express my special thanks to Mr.Rajesh Chaurasia, my colleague, for typing the entire manuscript.

Finally I thank all my friends on Facebook, my college mates, for encouraging me to write this book.

My heartfelt thanks, will not be complete unless I mention the big help I got from "Bhagvad Gita' and 'Google'.

You all are part of my these efforts BIG or SMALL.

# 1

Kiran's birth marked the union of Rajbala and Udayvir Singh, a learned headmaster residing in a North Indian village adjacent to his ancestral hometown. While Udayvir Singh possessed education, his mindset remained influenced by the prevailing norms of a deeply entrenched patriarchal society. Within this societal framework, various systems of oppression thrived, encompassing class divisions, racial biases, imperialistic remnants, and gender inequalities. The dominant fantasies of those governing this patriarchal order were not only allowed to persist but were actively encouraged.

Throughout Kiran's formative years, the weight of expectations burdened individuals, regardless of their gender or age. The laws that governed their lives were archaic, formulated by the elders two centuries prior, yet continued to be enforced by those seeking to retain their authority, despite their lack of relevance in contemporary society. Tragically, patriarchy had evolved into an entrenched way of life, vesting primary power in the hands of men. As a result, the women, comprising half of the nation's population, found themselves trapped in a distressing and deplorable predicament.

Denied deliberate opportunities for personal growth, freedom, and equal standing, women became victims of constant humiliation, torture, and exploitation. Although figures like Udayvir Singh and various statutory bodies attempted to ameliorate this dire situation, progress remained sluggish and fell far below the desired average.

Kiran was growing up quickly. The little girl's wings were gaining more and more flight every day. Both Udayvir Singh and Rajbala saw the self-confidence in Kiran, which brought them joy to watch. For the parents, Kiran was no longer the little girl cuddled on the couch with her mother at night. They were experiencing the pressure, expectations, and struggles of school, sports, and friends with Kiran. It was just the beginning. Rajbala used to say, "Kiran, you are growing up so fast, my baby. I wish I could slow down time. As I watch you sleep, your lips pout and move as if you are dreaming of taking a nice long drink of milk. You are getting bigger, doing more, needing me less, but you are still completely dependent on me."

Kiran and her younger brother were ensconced within the confines of their home, protected from the brutal realities of patriarchal Khap activities and their contentious edicts, which often prohibited marriages within the same Gotra (clan). The decisions handed down by the Khap Panchayat were oftentimes difficult to accept, imposing exorbitant fines and penalties, or even resulting in the untimely demise of the victim, or forcing them to commit suicide. In an effort to shield their daughter from such ruthless regulations, Udayvir Singh and Rajbala made the decision to keep her at a safe distance. Although Kiran was sheltered from these atrocities, her keen and inquisitive mind was acutely aware of the noxious effects of this society. Thus, Udayvir and Rajbala resolved to send Kiran to Delhi at the tender age of ten, to live with her aunt and uncle, Ajay Singh. In the company of cousins her own age, Kiran found solace and comfort.

# 2

Kiran's admission to the English Medium D.A.V. Junior College marked a significant turning point in her life, allowing her to break free from the clutches of the foolish and one-sided patriarchal society she had grown up in. Alongside her cousin Aryaman and Arya, Kiran found solace and liberation in this new educational environment. As time passed, Kiran embarked on a remarkable journey through various stages of formal education, commencing with early childhood education, progressing through primary schooling, and steadily advancing into secondary and tertiary education.

Despite her tender age of 15, Kiran displayed an impressive level of maturity and wisdom. Her father, recognizing her blossoming intellect, gifted her a diary on her 14th birthday, which became a vessel for documenting the significant events and reflections of her life thus far. Kiran possessed not only remarkable beauty but also a keen intelligence, often employing a creative approach to problem-solving. As she dedicated herself to her studies, she also took great care in nurturing her physical appearance, maintaining a balanced focus on both personal growth and outward appearance. Moreover, she demonstrated genuine concern and compassion for those around her, extending her kindness and support to both her family members at home and her peers at college.

While Kiran was generally obedient, she refused to grovel or bow down to unwarranted authority. She possessed the insight and sensibility of an intelligent young woman, even though she occasionally found herself at odds with her propensity for excessive talking in class. This particular trait, she discovered, was inherited from her mother, understanding that it was common among students. Kiran was fully aware of her own intelligence, but she struggled with a heightened sensitivity to criticism, often leaving her disheartened and discouraged.

In her quest for personal growth and empowerment, Kiran's journey continued to unfold, shaping her into a resilient and spirited individual who embraced her strengths while acknowledging her areas for improvement.

Now in the 10th standard, Kiran was becoming more curious about the world around her. No longer a child, she was now a teenager with many questions and a strong desire to find answers. For Kiran, this was a phase of life where her parents needed to shift gears in their parenting approach, as their teenager would soon be exposed to a whole new world full of opportunities and pitfalls. Fortunately, Kiran's maternal uncle, Ajay Singh, and his wife, Rajshree Singh, were always available to guide her. Uncle Ajay often advised Kiran and Arya with the quote, "The future belongs to those who believe in the beauty of their dreams. You both have to be authentic, you have to be true and you have to believe in yourselves." Kiran took her uncle's words to heart.

With her 10th Delhi board exams quickly approaching, Kiran was busy studying hard. She was nominated as class monitor and captain of the Red House, which gave her a sense of confidence and responsibility. After spending so many years at DAV, Kiran was now a confident dreamer, always thinking outside the box and striving for success. Every day, she grew into a better student, a better citizen, and an overall better person. She was the role model of the junior college.

They told him how proud they were of him and that his hard work and dedication had paid off. Kiran was overjoyed to see her father so happy and couldn't help but shed tears of happiness. She felt a sense of fulfillment and accomplishment, knowing that her efforts had paid off and that she had made her parents proud. Kiran's success not only brought happiness to her family, but also inspired her cousins and classmates to work harder and dream bigger.

As Kiran immersed herself in introspection, she came to a profound realization that her remarkable journey thus far owed its triumph not solely to her tireless efforts, but also to the boundless love and unwavering support bestowed upon her by her cherished family, particularly her guiding light, Uncle Ajay Singh. Deep within her heart, an overwhelming sense of gratitude welled up, acknowledging the myriad experiences and circumstances that had led her to this pivotal moment in her life, instilling within her a profound sense of appreciation for the transformative forces at play.

The resounding success she achieved in her 10th board examination served as a mere glimpse into the vast expanse of opportunities awaiting her in the future. Kiran, armed with her innate talent, unwavering determination, and an indomitable spirit, recognized that she possessed the potential to conquer any challenge she dared to undertake. It was this unwavering belief in her own abilities that fueled her aspirations, igniting a fierce determination to transcend boundaries and achieve greatness.

However, Kiran's unwavering confidence was not forged in isolation. She drew strength from the unwavering presence of her beloved family, a rock-solid support system that stood steadfastly by her side. Their unwavering faith in her abilities served as an anchor during moments of doubt, assuring her that she was never alone in her pursuit of dreams. Encircled by their unwavering love and support, Kiran felt a surge of confidence coursing through her veins, empowering her to fearlessly confront the vast expanse of the world that lay before her.

In the tapestry of her aspirations, Kiran's resolute determination intertwined harmoniously with the unconditional love of her family, forming a steadfast foundation upon which she could confidently tread her chosen path. The future beckoned, brimming with untold possibilities, and Kiran stood poised, ready to seize each and every opportunity that awaited her with unwavering tenacity and an open heart.

# 3

Embedded within the depths of time lies the timeless wisdom of the adage, "Time and Tide wait for none." This profound proverb serves as a poignant reminder of the immense value held by every fleeting moment, drawing a parallel between the relentless tides of the sea and the unstoppable passage of time. In light of this profound truth, it becomes imperative for us to seize the present and make the most of every precious second that graces our lives. This profound realization struck Kiran, a brilliant 12th Standard student, with newfound clarity as the approaching board examinations loomed on the horizon.

However, Kiran's journey towards academic excellence had commenced long before the specter of examinations cast its formidable shadow. She had approached her studies with unwavering dedication right from the onset of the school year, forging a path of scholarly pursuits that felt like a gentle breeze upon her determined spirit. Guided by her keen intellect, she sought out additional resources to enhance her understanding of the subjects at hand. Delving into the treasure troves of previous years' examination papers, she drew valuable insights from the wisdom captured within those well-worn pages. Yet, her quest for knowledge did not end there.

In this digital age, Kiran wisely harnessed the power of technology to augment her educational journey. She turned to the vast realm of YouTube, where a myriad of educational videos awaited her curious gaze. It was through these dynamic visual aids that she found herself immersed in a world of enriched comprehension, with complex concepts unraveling before her eyes. The interactive nature of these videos not only facilitated a deeper understanding but also served as a conduit for updated information, a valuable asset often absent from conventional textbooks and class notes. Kiran's exploration of these digital resources propelled her learning experience to new heights, empowering her to grasp the subjects with greater ease and finesse.

Armed with her meticulous study routine, coupled

with the wisdom gleaned from previous examination papers and the innovative insights found within the realm of online educational platforms, Kiran navigated her academic journey with a sense of purpose and mastery. The sands of time, once seemingly unforgiving, now appeared more pliable in her capable hands. With every passing day, she solidified her foundation of knowledge, inching ever closer to the summit of academic success, undeterred by the relentless march of time.

In this symphony of knowledge acquisition, Kiran discovered that time need not be an adversary to be feared but rather a companion to be embraced. With each moment she invested wisely in her studies, she fortified herself against the ebb and flow of life's tides, emerging as a resilient and accomplished scholar poised to conquer the challenges that lay ahead.

One of Kiran's professors suggested a unique method of teaching, where she would team up with her cousin sister, Arya. The duo split the syllabus in half so that each would master one part and then teach it to the other. Although this system added an extra layer of pressure on Arya and Kiran, it was ultimately a positive form of pressure, as they both followed the system to great success. Kiran was a vivacious and adventurous girl who loved life and lived in the moment. Although she was going through an exciting period of transition from adolescence to teenagehood, she never let her curiosity and inquisitiveness veer towards sexual experimentation, unlike many of her peers. Kiran maintained a personal diary, which was off-limits to others.

One entry from her diary reads, 'Being away from home and my family is hard. I used to dread the idea of leaving home and cherish my freedom there, but now that I'm out here, the reality is harsh. Sometimes, I just start crying alone. Whenever my mom calls and asks if I've eaten, I lie and tell her I've had a full meal. Being in a new city with no close friends has made me feel extremely lonely. Although my uncle, aunt, and cousins are affectionate and caring, I've come to appreciate my parents even more. I realize now just how much they love me. But I won't give up and go back home because I'm here to fulfill their dreams.'

Deeply ingrained within Kiran's consciousness was the profound understanding that the elusive elixir of success required an unwavering commitment to hard work, an unyielding dedication to the task at hand, and an unwavering determination to give her very best, regardless of the outcome. As the final examinations of her 12th Standard education drew nearer with each passing day, a palpable sense of urgency permeated the air, urging her to delve deeper into her studies. The ticking clock and the mounting pressure posed a formidable challenge, but Kiran remained resolute, unswerving in her focus and determination.

In this crucial juncture of her academic journey, Kiran found solace and unwavering support from her ever-present mother. Throughout her preparatory days leading up to the exams, her mother stood as a pillar of strength, a constant source of encouragement and guidance. With wisdom earned through life's ups and downs, her mother instilled within Kiran the belief that no obstacle was insurmountable, and the notion of surrender was anathema to her indomitable spirit. This maternal bond served as a beacon of resilience, empowering Kiran to confront challenges head-on, fortified by the unwavering love and support that enveloped her.

When the long-awaited day arrived, and the 12th Standard examination results were unveiled, an extraordinary achievement awaited Kiran. In a stunning display of academic prowess, she emerged as an unparalleled trailblazer, achieving a perfect score of 100% in every subject. This monumental feat etched her name indelibly in the annals of the Delhi board's history, forever marking her as the highest scorer ever recorded. The echoes of her accomplishment reverberated far and wide, a testament to her unwavering dedication and unwavering pursuit of excellence.

Now, standing at the precipice of boundless possibilities, Kiran found herself at the crossroads of her future, brimming with anticipation and excitement. The world beckoned, offering a myriad of paths leading to a fulfilling professional life. With her remarkable achievements as a testament to her capabilities, Kiran now faced the task of deciding which road to embark upon, armed with the knowledge that her tireless efforts had laid a foundation for success that would guide her towards a future brimming with opportunities and fulfillment.

# 4

With the results of her 12th Standard now in, Kiran found herself at a crossroads - faced with the all-important decision of what to do next. With countless career paths to choose from, Kiran was filled with doubt, despite receiving wonderful advice from her friends and family. Unlike most, she had no interest in pursuing the traditional career paths of an engineer, doctor or business professional. Instead, Kiran was a bird with different coloured feathers who had her sights set on a career in teaching - a profession that could be successful in both government and private schools, colleges, and universities. Her aim was to obtain an honors programme that would be beneficial to both society and herself.

Teaching, renowned as one of the most esteemed and revered professions on a global scale, stands tall with its enticing blend of lucrative earning potential and an unparalleled reputation that resonates across borders. As the education system expands at a rapid pace, the demand for skilled educators has soared to unprecedented heights, manifesting in an exponential surge of enticing employment opportunities within this dynamic sector. The allure of teaching, with its ability to shape young minds and leave an indelible impact on future generations, captured Kiran's imagination, setting her on a path of contemplation and reflection.

An inspirational figure who played a pivotal role in Kiran's career considerations was Anand Kumar, the visionary behind the esteemed Super 30 Programme. An embodiment of dedication and excellence, Anand Kumar's remarkable journey ignited a spark within Kiran, driving her to explore the realm of teaching as a means to honor her father's legacy and continue his noble work. Guided by this profound influence, Kiran embarked upon a profound self-assessment, meticulously weighing the merits and drawbacks of pursuing a career in teaching against the myriad of other tantalizing professional paths that beckoned her.

In her meticulous examination of the pros and cons, Kiran endeavored to unravel the multifaceted layers of teaching, seeking to unearth the untold treasures that lie within. The allure of imparting knowledge, molding young minds, and shaping the future of society were among the undeniable advantages that propelled Kiran towards this noble calling. The intrinsic satisfaction derived from witnessing the growth and development of her students, coupled with the gratification of making a lasting impact, stood as pillars of motivation in her deliberations.

Yet, Kiran was acutely aware of the challenges that teaching posed, the potential sacrifices it demanded, and the arduous journey it entailed. The rigorous demands of managing diverse student needs, navigating administrative complexities, and the occasional emotional toll were aspects that warranted thoughtful consideration. In her quest for a fulfilling professional path, Kiran meticulously examined the alternative career options that enticed her, assessing their promises and pitfalls with discerning eyes.

Armed with an analytical mindset and a commitment to charting a course that aligned with her aspirations, Kiran sought to strike a delicate balance between her passions, her father's legacy, and the prospects that awaited her. As she meticulously weighed the scales of possibility, she recognized that teaching held an undeniable allure, driven by its ability to touch lives, inspire change, and carve a lasting legacy.

In the grand tapestry of her life's choices, the decision to embrace teaching emerged as a canvas upon which Kiran could paint her father's memory, intertwining it with her own journey of growth and fulfillment. With each passing moment of contemplation, her resolve solidified, setting the stage for her to embark on a path that resonated deeply within her soul, carrying forth her father's legacy while crafting a remarkable professional voyage that would leave an indelible mark upon the world.

Ultimately, Kiran decided that teaching was the path for her. She believed that teachers have the opportunity and potential to transform lives, and that teaching offered the chance to be continuously creative, to continuously improve, and to make a difference in a student's life every single day. With this in mind, Kiran enrolled in Jawahar Lal Nehru (JNU) and obtained a mandatory Master's Degree in Hindi Literature with 80% marks, as well as passing the National Eligibility Test (NET) and Delhi State Level Eligibility Test (SLAT). She also learned the art of expressing her thoughts before dignitaries, and was capable of understanding new and creative ways of teaching.

Kiran cleared all the hurdles and attained the required educational qualifications and administrative knowledge, eventually becoming an Assistant Professor at JNU. She even enrolled in a doctoral degree programme, with her research thesis focusing on "What's missing in Valmiki Ramayana and RamcharitManas of Tulsidas". Due to her academic aptitude and general abilities, the university entrusted Kiran with various duties, such as overseeing student admissions, developing class syllabi and course materials, and teaching and supervising graduate and postgraduate students. Additionally, she was responsible for preparing and conducting examinations, evaluating exam papers, training and mentoring junior teaching faculty, participating in departmental faculty and committee meetings, and writing and publishing research reports, papers, articles, and books. Although her workload was considerable, Kiran was happy and satisfied with her professional growth, as well as the time available for her personal grooming on Saturdays/ Sundays and summer and winter vacations.

Beyond her professional accomplishments, Kiran was also guiding her cousin sister Arya, who was also pursuing a career in teaching Hindi up to the 12th standard. Despite her youth, Kiran was widely respected as the youngest professor in her department, an epitome of kindness, empathy, and a great teacher. She was much more than her credentials, experience, and intelligence - she was a kind, compassionate, positive, and inspiring teacher, and had become quite popular at just 25 years of age. She was generally perceived as a woman with both beauty and brains, truly an exceptional individual.

## 5

Kiran was graced with the privilege of being invited as the Chief Guest to address the students of Sainik School on their annual day function. Her attire was an embodiment of elegance as she wore a stunning saree with a traditional design that exuded grace and charm. Kiran was aware of the cultural significance of the saree, but she never hesitated to experiment with western outfits.

Upon her arrival, Captain Abhimanyu Singh, the coordinator of the event, welcomed her with open arms. As a serving captain of the EME division of the Indian Army, Captain Singh aimed to inspire the young minds present at the event. During his opening speech, he expressed his gratitude towards Kiran for accepting their invitation and becoming the Chief Guest of the event. Captain Singh highlighted Kiran's remarkable achievements as a professor of Hindi in the renowned Jawaharlal Nehru University under Delhi administration. He mentioned that even though Kiran had completed her postgraduate and research in Hindi, she had the exceptional ability to articulate her thoughts fluently in English.

Captain Singh praised Kiran's achievements in the fields of education, literature, and administration. He commended her philanthropic efforts and her selfless service to society.

He further added that Kiran had influenced the lives of numerous students and had left an indelible mark on their lives. Captain Singh expressed his gratitude to all the parents, students, and teachers for their presence at the event, and he thanked the staff for their contributions to make the ceremony worthwhile.

Throughout his speech, Captain Singh's eyes were fixated on Kiran. Eyes are known to be the windows to one's soul, and it was evident that Captain Singh's admiration for Kiran was profound. Kiran, in turn, expressed her gratitude towards Captain Singh and thanked him for his kind words.

Kiran then addressed the students and highlighted the importance of education beyond just acquiring information. She emphasized the need for students to become aware of their responsibility towards protecting the environment and learning new technologies. She commended the school for its achievements and acknowledged the impact it had on thousands of lives. Kiran urged the students to work hard and strive to make the school and the nation proud, just like Captain Singh had done.

Kiran said, "Thank you so much Captain Abhimanyu Singh who has spared no adjectives to describe a simple person like me. It gives me immense pleasure to be here this evening and to address the young students of the Sainik School on the occasion of its Annual Day function.

"Education is not just the amount of information that is put into a child's brain undigested, unrelated, and unassimilated. Students should be made aware of their responsibility and duty towards protecting nature and learning new technology. Your school has made many accomplishments and has impacted thousands of lives for good or better. Only 1 percent of the people on the planet get what you have got in this school so please give yourself a big, big round of applause.

"You are the future of this great nation and many of you would become Captain Abhimanyu. You all are smart, good looking, and dedicated. Please work hard and make this school and nation proud, the same way as Captain Abhimanyu Singh is doing.

"Thanks a million to the parents, students, teachers, and other staff for giving me this much respect. Captain, you are so sweet, and our country is in safe hands because of soldiers like you."

As the resounding echoes of Kiran's speech gradually dissipated into the air, she extended her heartfelt gratitude to the distinguished gathering that graced the event with their presence. With a genuine warmth in her voice, she expressed her sincere appreciation for the respect and unwavering support bestowed upon her by each individual in attendance. This collective embrace of camaraderie and encouragement served as a pillar of strength, propelling her forward on her path of aspirations and endeavors.

Amidst the sea of attendees, one figure stood tall, commanding both admiration and reverence — Captain Singh, a paragon of dedication and selflessness in service to the nation. Kiran's words swelled with profound admiration as she paid tribute to this gallant soldier, whose unwavering commitment to safeguarding the country left an indelible mark upon her heart. She expressed her unwavering belief that under the watchful eyes and courageous leadership of individuals like Captain Singh, the nation remained secure, fortified by their valor and unwavering resolve.

In her eloquent expression of gratitude and unwavering belief in the nation's safeguarding, Kiran's words resonated with a profound sense of conviction and reassurance. As she concluded her speech, a sense of unity and shared purpose enveloped the room, reminding everyone present of the collective responsibility to support and uphold the nation's defenders. Together, they stood as a testament to the indomitable spirit of unity, honor, and respect that permeated every facet of society, forging a stronger bond between the citizenry and those who selflessly protect and serve.

# *6*

In the realm of fleeting encounters, Abhimanyu's rendezvous with Kiran spanned a mere two hours, an ephemeral interlude that nonetheless etched an indelible impression upon his consciousness. The memory of that brief exchange lingered with a vibrancy that defied time's inexorable march, provoking profound contemplation within his heart. Could this, he wondered, be the advent of love at first sight, a notion he had once regarded with skepticism? As he delved deeper into the recesses of his mind, Abhimanyu discovered a wealth of knowledge, gleaned from books that revealed a scientific explanation behind the enigmatic sensation of instant infatuation. Although the depths of profound love had yet to be traversed in their nascent connection, Kiran had effortlessly woven herself into the tapestry of his memories, casting an enchanting spell that mirrored the enchantment of falling in love.

In his solitary musings, Abhimanyu embarked upon a logical exploration, contemplating the plausibility of love at first sight manifesting within the confines of his own existence. An intellectual introspection beckoned him to unravel the intricacies of this captivating phenomenon, acknowledging that the path to love's enduring embrace may be laden with intricate challenges. Despite his initial reservations, the sheer force of attraction he experienced upon encountering Kiran stirred a cascade of ethereal butterflies within, confirming the tantalizing possibility that love's enigmatic tendrils had taken hold. The incredulity of his own fortune seemed unfathomable, yet the essence of his being yearned to unravel the enigma that was Kiran, an insatiable thirst for knowledge gnawing at his soul.

In this moment of awakening, Abhimanyu acknowledged the dichotomy between the initial spark of attraction and the daunting task of sustaining a profound connection. The flame of love, kindled in those fleeting moments, demanded constant nurturing to withstand the trials that lay ahead. He embraced the realization that the journey from love's nascent beginnings to its enduring embodiment demanded unwavering dedication and an unwavering commitment to mutual growth. And so, with each passing moment, Abhimanyu's determination grew, fueled by an insatiable desire to explore the depths of Kiran's being, to uncover the intricacies of her soul, and to weave a tapestry of shared experiences that would transcend the boundaries of time.

In the vast expanse of possibilities, Abhimanyu found himself caught in a delicate dance between skepticism and surrender. Love, in all its myriad hues, had bestowed upon him a precious gift — the opportunity to immerse himself in a connection that defied conventional understanding. And as his heart intertwined with Kiran's, the tendrils of affection gradually unfolded, unfurling a profound narrative that promised to traverse the realms of attraction, understanding, and unwavering devotion.

Abhimanyu, by nature, was a shy person, and he was now facing an internal conflict as to whether he should contact Kiran or let this question die within him. There was no commitment from either of them, yet Abhimanyu had developed a sense of desperate attachment to her. It was the joy of being together for a short while, coupled with the fear of losing each other, that plagued him. He constantly wondered if there was any sort of relationship between him and Kiran.

Feeling like a teenager, Abhimanyu believed he had fallen in love with Kiran. The situation was more complex and compelling than anything he had known before. He was immature and hardly understood any aspect of love except for a strong urge for sexual attraction, mutual enjoyment, physical affection, friendship, and romantic excitement.

Abhimanyu found himself standing at a crossroads where he was only speculating about love at first sight, without even the slightest idea of Kiran's point of view. He was not sure if Kiran even knew about his feelings. Was he experiencing being in love with someone who didn't love him back? It could very well be the case, and Abhimanyu thought that one-sided love would be painful. However, he believed that this should not stop him from loving Kiran every single day.

As an army soldier, he decided to talk about it with Kiran. He knew that having a conversation with her about how he felt might be frightening, but it was often the best way.

# 7

Abhimanyu arrived at Café Coffee Day in Connaught Place at precisely 4:30 PM. He had dressed in an ultra-white shirt, gray trousers, and brown, nicely polished shoes, a combination that perfectly complemented his tall, handsome frame and army-style hair. Abhimanyu was a naturally good-looking man, and he was ecstatic and brimming with excitement at the mere thought of meeting Kiran. He had even arranged a bouquet of opulent purple flowers to present to her. When he spotted Kiran entering the café, his heart soared. He rushed to the entrance to catch a glimpse of her and welcome her inside.

Kiran was a vision of beauty with her sculpted, twine-thin figure, tapered waist, and burnished complexion. Her arched eyebrows framed sweeping eyelashes, and her well-carved features were accentuated by big lotus eyes. Her flowing moon-shadow black hair was a pleasure to behold, and she had enticing constellation black eyes that shone above her puffy, heart-shaped lips, which looked as sweet as strawberries. Kiran's bouncy personality and sugary voice made her a subject of adoration and envy for all who knew her. Her vibrant clothing added to her allure, and her luminous perfection and million-dollar smile made it nearly impossible for the males in and around the café to take their eyes off her. According to Abhimanyu, Kiran was the most glamorous woman he had ever seen, and she carried herself with elegance and grace. Her cute dimples, nice doe eyes, toned body, and decent hair made her the darling of Abhimanyu, who was momentarily dumbfounded and amazed by her beauty. He didn't know where to start, but he managed to point towards two cozy corner chairs.

"Abhi, what's so special today that you wanted me to come here? Is it your birthday?" Kiran asked as she settled into the cozy corner chair.

"No, I have already answered you," Abhi replied. "Let me give you my background. I am a serving Indian Army Officer. My father, Col. Ranjit Singh, was also in the Indian Army. My mother, Mrs. Veermati

Singh, has been an army wife. I have a brother, Aditya Singh, two years younger than me who is aspiring to be an agriculture scientist. We live in Gurugram, and we have our ancestral village and agricultural land in Hasangarh under Rohtak district."

Kiran listened attentively, then shared her own background. "I come from a rural farming background. My father, Shri Udayvir Singh, is a retired Headmaster. My mother, Rajbala Singh, is a homemaker. They are staying in Bhagwanpur, which falls in Meerut District. My parents sent me to Delhi to protect me from those draconian laws of Khap Panchayat at an early age. Since then, I have been brought up by my maternal uncle, Ajay Singh, and aunt, Rajshree Singh, along with my cousins Arya and Aryaman, almost of my age. I have studied in JNU and am now a professor in the same university."

Abhi nodded. "Glad to know that we hail from a similar background. I appreciate your efforts to reach this milestone from a humble background. It must be really tough."

"It was," Kiran agreed.

Abhi ordered coffee with samosas for both of them. "What are your likes and interests apart from books? Do you go for movies, dramas or shopping?"

"I have seen almost all the Hindi movies with my

cousin sister Arya. I like men in uniform, especially the olive green and their disciplined life," Kiran said, smiling.

Abhi smiled back. "At least, I have one such quality of wearing olive green. Apart from the regular army duties, I am good at Tennis and Badminton."

"I like sports, except the game of cricket," Kiran said. "I love Hockey for its speed and art of tackling the opponents."

Abhi then asked, "Can I invite your parents sometimes in our officer's mess for dinner?"

"My parents are based in our village. They rarely come here," Kiran replied. "I am a bit apprehensive in asking my maternal Uncle and Aunty for dinner."

"Can I ask you a personal question if you permit?" Abhi asked.

Kiran nodded. "Please go ahead."

"How do you manage your reading, teaching, and research work in addition to your personal grooming?" Abhi asked. "According to me, you are very beautiful and a rare combination of beauty and brains."

Kiran blushed slightly. "I really strive to achieve the goals set by me for research and teaching. Other things you observed are a result of your kindness. Some answers will need time as it is too early, Abhi, to accept or reject your observations. Can only say, "You are a wonderful man."

Kiran finished her coffee and stood up. "I would like to leave now. Thanks for your wonderful hospitality and lovely flowers. The fragrance stays with me."

# 8

Abhimanyu was acutely aware that his impatience could have a direct effect on his chances with Kiran. She wasn't officially his partner yet, and he knew that building a successful relationship required patience. But despite his efforts to control his frustration and anxiety, he found himself growing increasingly impatient with Kiran's inability to reciprocate his feelings immediately. He didn't want to react impulsively and risk alienating her or making her feel rejected. So instead of confronting her directly, he decided to send her a text.

"Dear Kiran," he began. "I never knew the meaning of love till the day I met you. Having you as my sweetheart is like a dream come true. I get nervous and speechless whenever I think of sharing my feelings in front of you. So I decided to pen them down. I want to let you know that you are my angel, my true companion, my best friend and my soulmate. I want to tell you that I love you till eternity. I am madly in love with your gentle smile, sparkling eyes, your warm touch and essence of the bond we share. I cherish each and every moment I spend with you. You are the most precious thing in my life. My love for you is something I'll never run out of. There are no words to describe the love I feel for you. It's unwavering, tender and boundless. There is nowhere else I would rather go than be by your side with your hand in mine. In a world where so many things can be uncertain, you are one thing that I will always be certain of. It started with a dream of a life together and the dreams only got better. We have a wonderful memory together, I wish to spend my entire life with you. Sincerely in love, Your's ABHI."

Kiran read the message over and over, her emotions in turmoil. With each passing sentence, she felt a confusing mix of anxiety, ecstasy, fear, and shock. Her palms grew clammy and her feet turned cold as she struggled to process the intensity of Abhimanyu's words. She was angry with him for being so presumptuous, yet she couldn't help but be moved by the depth of his emotions.

She confided in her cousin sister, Arya, who was amused by the whole situation. "What caste does he belong to?" Arya asked, her practicality taking over. "Our families are considering so many suitable boys for you and me, including research scholars, professors, top-notch doctors, and engineers. Why waste your time with an army man?"

Arya looked at her younger sister Kiran with curiosity. "Why do you have a soft corner for Abhimanyu?" she asked.

Without a second thought, Kiran replied, "I love his personality. His etiquettes are impeccable, and he has a deep respect for women. He knows how to surprise me and make me feel special all the time. I feel secure when he's around, and his five-minute phone calls brighten up my entire day. He's lively, and no other guy dares to look at me when I'm with him. He loves passionately and is always loyal to me. Plus, he belongs to our caste, so our families will surely be more accepting of him."

Arya felt proud of her sister and her potential boyfriend. She advised Kiran to respond to Abhimanyu's message without giving up too much and eventually take both families into confidence. Kiran agreed to respond to Abhi's message and inform her maternal uncle, aunt, and her own parents.

She replied, "Dear Abhi, I admire the way you share

your dreams and wishes with me. I'm still not confident enough to feel and express our love for each other, but be assured that my love for you will only grow with time. I might not let you lock your fingers with mine, but these little things make me feel deeper in love with you. I wake up thinking about you and fall asleep with thoughts of you. There's one word of caution for you: 'Please do not beg for love, just demand it.'"

Though Kiran's feelings remain unexpressed, Abhi understood them through her glittery eyes.

ABHI WAS OVER THE MOON.

# 9

As their tale unfolded, Kiran began to ponder the depth of Abhi's affection for her, and so she decided to meet him once more before revealing their love to their families. Her heart yearned for a bit of whimsy and adventure, so she decided to surprise Abhi with something out of the ordinary, just as he had surprised her many times before.

Abhi was a man of sensitivity and responsibility, and he knew that just hearing Kiran's voice over the phone wouldn't be enough. He longed to see her radiant face once more and feel her warmth in person. Summoning all his courage, he sent her a text message, inviting her for a high tea at a restaurant near JNU at 8 PM that evening, after their classes had ended. As he waited for her response, he knew that he needed to see her, just as a blind person needs two eyes to see.

Kiran accepted his invitation, and Abhi arrived half an hour early, as was customary for an army man. He sat at a corner table with a bouquet of flowers, waiting for Kiran. When she arrived, she was a vision of beauty in a white Punjabi suit and colorful Rajasthani shoes. Her loose, silky hair and radiant, milky skin made her look like an angel that had descended to earth on a full moon night.

As Abhi tried to avoid staring at her, he couldn't help but be drawn in by her beauty, and Kiran knew it. They ordered some mouth-watering vegetarian dishes and Abhi began to recount a story with childlike innocence, as they both savored the delicious food and each other's company.

Kiran's eyes widened in surprise as she processed Abhi's words. "I was not prepared to face this unexpected situation," she replied, her voice shaking slightly. "I need some space. I don't want to dishearten you too."

Abhi took a deep breath, his eyes never leaving Kiran's face. "It has taken a lot of courage to tell you and my parents, though it was scary," he said. "I understand that you need time, but please know that I am serious about this."

Kiran looked at Abhi, her heart heavy with conflicting emotions. "I have shared my feelings and emotions with you," she said slowly, "but this doesn't mean that I have ever given you a blanket confirmation that I love you. But yes, I care about you. Please give me time to get the blessings of my parents for this relationship."

Abhi nodded, his expression one of understanding. "I have another twenty days before I move to Ambala for the new posting," he said. "We will meet soon."

They finished their meal in a comfortable silence, stealing glances at each other every now and then. As they said their goodbyes, both of them were filled with a sense of anticipation for what the future might hold.

# 10

Seated at the well-laid dinner table, Abhi found himself immersed in the delightful flavors of his mother's culinary creations. The aromatic Rice Pulao, warm Rotis, luscious Black Dal, refreshing Raita, and the crowning glory of Kheer, his cherished dessert, tantalized his taste buds with each delectable bite. Gratitude washed over him as he savored the symphony of flavors, appreciating the love and care his mother poured into every dish.

Meanwhile, the inquisitive nature of Abhi's mother, Veermati Singh, had been ignited by the mention of a certain girl named Kiran. Intrigued by the mere mention of this enigmatic figure in her son's life, she seized the moment while his father was away for a leisurely stroll to satisfy her curiosity.

As Abhi found himself in the unexpected spotlight of his mother's questioning, he realized he couldn't evade her persistent inquiries. Reluctantly, he began to unravel the tapestry of his relationship with Kiran, painting a vivid picture of her as a remarkable Jat girl hailing from the vibrant city of Delhi, carrying with her an admirable background.

On the other side of the equation, Kiran grappled with her own battle to find the courage necessary to divulge the existence of her relationship with Abhi to her parents. Gathering around the family dinner table, she mustered the strength within herself to share the news that had been weighing on her heart.

"Dad, I have a boyfriend," she announced, her voice filled with a mix of trepidation and determination, bracing herself for the impending reaction.

To her immense surprise, her parents met her revelation with a composed demeanor, displaying an unexpected sense of acceptance and understanding. Their calm reaction gave way to an openness to meet Abhi and his family, an invitation extended with genuine interest. The younger members of the family radiated joy, their hearts dancing with excitement. Kiran, in that moment, felt a tremendous sense of relief, gratitude flooding her being as she realized the depth of her parents' acceptance and support.

In a beautiful twist of fate, both Abhi and Kiran had summoned the strength to conquer their inner fears and take a resolute step forward in their relationship. The journey, though still unfolding, held promise and potential, their hearts entwined in a bond that transcended the uncertainties and anxieties they had once harbored. As they sat at their respective dinner tables, experiencing the tapestry of emotions woven into each moment, they embraced the power of love and acceptance, poised to navigate the intricacies of their evolving connection.

# 11

Marriage was a milestone that held great significance in the life of every individual. It was a goal that parents aspired for their children to achieve, as having a suitable life partner was not only a matter of personal satisfaction, but also a social security for the family. Parents felt a sense of moral responsibility to settle their children's social life, and some children, while choosing their life partners themselves, still involved their parents in the traditional and beautiful customs and rituals of the relationship.

As the first step in this journey, both Kiran and Abhimanyu's families decided to match their horoscopes. An expert fortune teller was called upon to undertake this enigmatic research and development, and both Kiran and Abhimanyu were requested not to participate in the process.

"Kiran, do you believe in all this?" Abhimanyu asked as they sat together in the living room, thinking about their horoscope discussions.

"Not 100 percent, but what is the harm in knowing it and satisfying our parents?" Kiran replied with a shrug.

Abhimanyu furrowed his brow. "What if they don't match?"

Kiran chuckled. "I'll go as per the fortune teller's advice, jokingly."

"I do not trust all this, even if they don't match one percent," Abhimanyu said firmly. "I am not going to leave you."

"Neither am I, Abhi," Kiran reassured him. "Why do you become panicky so fast? Have trust in yourself, and if not, at least trust me."

"Sure, na! If that is the case, let us enjoy the entire exercise," Abhimanyu relented.

As they completed the ritual, Kiran was deemed strong-headed but always correct, while Abhimanyu was intense and passionate, making him a man of surrender, acceptance, and inner focus on sacrifice and growth. "Thank God there wasn't anything abnormal," they both thought, relieved.

The families of Ranjit Singh and Udayvir Singh were brimming with joy as they met at the sprawling farmhouse of Col. Virendra Singh, a close friend of Ranjit Singh. The picturesque venue, located on the outskirts of Rohtak, provided the perfect backdrop for a night of celebration. Col. Virendra Singh played the perfect host, treating his guests to a lavish dinner. His son, Abhinandan Singh, a promising young lawyer, had meticulously planned the arrangements for the feast and accommodation.

As they indulged in the sumptuous fare, Arya's gaze fell upon a book titled "Winning Strategy by Martin and Laflay" lying on the side table. She was so engrossed in the book that she didn't realize a handsome man had taken a seat beside her. Abhinandan introduced himself to Arya, and soon they were engrossed in an animated conversation, oblivious to the world around them.

Their lively interaction did not go unnoticed by Kiran and Abhimanyu. Abhi suggested, "How about we rope in these two for a joint wedding ceremony along with ours?" Kiran and Abhi approached Arya and Abhinandan, and the idea was well-received by both.

The proposal was discussed with the highest level of the families, including Udayvir Singh, Rajbala Singh, Ajay Singh, Rajshree, Col. Ranjit Singh, and

Veermati Singh. Everyone was elated at the thought of the weddings being conducted on the same day, at the same venue. Col. Ranjit Singh exclaimed, "This is great! We will be friends and relatives now." The decision was made to hold the ceremony six months later when Abhi returned home for a month's leave after joining his army assignment in Ambala.

Abhinandan's relationship with Arya was described by Abhimanyu as "Buy One, Get One Free," and Arya smiled and thanked him and Kiran for the suggestion. The elders unanimously decided to wait until Abhi's return to hold the ceremony, allowing the young couple to enjoy their courtship for a few more months.

# 12

As per schedule, Abhi departed after a week but was redirected to Pathankot instead of Ambala for a specific and undisclosed duty. Although it was business as usual for Abhi's parents, Kiran found it emotionally devastating as she knew the sensitive areas Abhi would be posted to. Nevertheless, she was proud of her fiancé's supreme duty to defend the country against any enemy invasion or terrorist intrusion. Tears trickled down her cheeks as Abhimanyu turned away from his home gate. After all, Abhi was a selfless soldier who prioritized the nation's interest over his own.

Captain Abhimanyu Singh was assigned specific responsibilities such as Mission Planning, Leader Development, and the development of policies and procedures. As per the military code, the quickest way to know if an officer is good is during combat. Abhi was chosen to lead the troops in combat and fight to win the nation's land wars. Additionally, he was entrusted with the responsibility of logistics to eliminate high-value targets of terrorists.

Being an army officer's girlfriend or fiancée is a unique experience. Every news article about the armed forces, especially in the area where he is posted, grabs your attention right away. Even though you are miles apart, he is always the first to know of your sadness and joy. His love and support make it all worthwhile. Kiran has gone days without hearing his voice and months without seeing him, but this only strengthens her love and pride for him. She daydreams about how her entire schedule and priorities would change when he comes home on leave.

Abhimanyu was advised to go to Ladakh due to movement by Chinese troops near the India-Pakistan-China border. He was there for ten days, where altitudes ranged from high to super high, snowfall could reach up to 40 feet, and temperatures dropped to -30 to -40 degrees Celsius. The wind chill factor made matters worse for Abhimanyu and his troops. Communication was a serious concern, but as nothing was abnormal, Abhi's troops scaled back to their base camp, which fell under the peace zone for the time being. Abhimanyu called his parents to let them know he was okay and then called Kiran.

Abhi's voice crackled through the phone as he spoke, "I missed you in ways that not even words can understand. The day is not very far, one day when there will be no distance between you and me."

Kiran's response was soft, "We are the perfect couple. We are just not in a perfect situation."

Abhi chuckled, "What's something that often reminds you of me? Romance is a vital part of every healthy relationship and you most of the time try to overlook that."

Kiran smirked, "Your dialogue that 'A man and a horse never get old for marriage or union or mating', but when I see you on Skype, you are becoming hotter day by day. Shall I tell you what happened to me last night?"

Abhi eagerly replied, "It sounds interesting. I can't wait anymore."

Kiran began, "I was sleeping last night with a thought that it has been years spent without you. I was lonely and it was raining at sporadic intervals. I could hear some dreadful thunder after lightning. All of sudden, I felt your presence on the other side of my bed. I opened my eyes, saw nothing but I could feel a kind of warmth and you were sleeping for the rest of the moments. I slid over into the warm pocket of warmth and cozy comfort."

Abhi gasped, "Exactly the same thing happened with me and I felt that we were sleeping together that too under the chilled life threatening conditions at Ladakh. Ever since you have come into my life, every moment I live is like a moment spent in heaven. I have never felt so alive in life. I love you."

Kiran's voice was full of affection, "You are my first thought in the morning and my very last thought at night. What do you want me to do next time I see you?"

Abhi replied with conviction, "Next time I see you, I am going to wrap my arms around you, kiss you and never let you go."

Kiran teased, "What exactly are you doing right now?"

Abhi's voice turned serious, "Right now, I am exploring the Jungles for terrorists hideout. One day I want to explore your body like a map. I'll start with your lips and don't really know where I go all the way down."

Kiran sighed, "Abhi, you get so involved with me in being dirty in long distance conversations that you forget you stay in very sensitive areas and the enemies' bullets do not discriminate in war zones."

Every relationship has its ebbs and flows, its peaks and valleys, and it's not always sunshine and rainbows. Kiran and Abhimanyu were acutely aware of this fact, and despite their love for each other, they still experienced bouts of loneliness. The timing of their conversations was a major issue, but they persisted with their trust and commitment to each other, which only strengthened their bond.

On the other hand, Arya and Abhinandan were enjoying the thrills of romance and physical intimacy. They had the freedom to meet anywhere in Delhi, be it a cozy restaurant or a bustling movie theater. They often acted like a married couple, even though they were not legally bound.

Abhinandan, being a lawyer, would often cite the court's view that a live-in relationship falls within the ambit of the right to life enshrined under Article 21 of the Indian Constitution. Even though they were not living together, their meetings were considered akin to a live-in relationship. They engaged in minor flirting, and Arya would explain to him that while it may not be illegal, it was considered immoral by society.

Abhinandan's views on casual sex were not uncommon in metro cities like Delhi, and they often argued about the morality of their actions. However, they continued to indulge in casual sex whenever the opportunity arose, unlike Kiran and Abhimanyu, who were miles apart in a long-distance relationship. Arya never divulged the full extent of her physical relationship with Abhinandan to Kiran.

# 13

Abhimanyu finally returned to Delhi after 11 long months, and the excitement amongst his family and loved ones was palpable. The parents of Abhimanyu, Kiran, Abhinandan, and Arya eagerly awaited the big celebrations that were to come. The four of them gathered at a posh restaurant in Hauz Khas, South Delhi to share a meal together, reminiscing about Abhimanyu's time in the Army and discussing Abhinandan Singh's unconventional cohabitation relationship with Arya. As they sat together, they all hoped for something magical to happen, something that would allow them to commit to each other and let their love and respect grow even stronger.

As if by some stroke of luck, the parents suddenly

woke from their slumber and realized that this was the perfect opportunity to arrange the marriages of Abhimanyu and Kiran, and Abhinandan and Arya, in accordance with essential rituals and the sanctity of a Hindu wedding. The weddings were set to take place on the 15th of the month, as dictated by the position of the stars and the religious advice of their family Pandit. No longer were the days when grooms rode on horses while the Baratis danced and threw currency notes.

The grandeur of the wedding ceremonies unfolded across a series of blissful days, hosted within the illustrious premises of the Ashoka Hotel, a cherished gem in the tapestry of India Tourism Development Corporation, Delhi. This regal setting served as the perfect backdrop to honor the ancestral roots that both brides proudly hailed from, weaving together the threads of their shared heritage.

Immersed in reverence and devotion, the couple paid homage to the sacred customs that held profound significance in their religious traditions. Every ritual meticulously observed, they embarked on a journey of spiritual union, guided by the age-old customs that bound their souls. In the creation of a sacred space, adorned with fragrant blooms and divine symbols, they kindled the Sacred Fire, an emblem of purity and divine blessings.

As the exchange of garlands united their hearts in a colorful tapestry of love, they absorbed themselves in the joy of taking the Seven Sacred Steps, a pledge to walk hand in hand through the twists and turns of life's sacred path. Beyond the core wedding ceremony, a kaleidoscope of festivities unfolded, each marked by its unique charm and significance.

The engagement ceremony, a shimmering prelude to their eternal bond, symbolized the blossoming of their commitment. The mehendi ceremony painted their hands and hearts with intricate patterns, a celebration of artistry and auspicious beginnings. The sangeet ceremony filled the air with melodious melodies and jubilant dances, the collective voice of loved ones harmonizing their joy.

The tilak/sagai ceremony, an affectionate exchange of blessings, sealed the bond between the families, fortifying their union. The haldi ceremony, a radiant embrace of turmeric's vibrant hues, bestowed blessings of good fortune and radiant beauty upon the couple. The poignant moment of *kanyadaan*, where the bride's hand was lovingly placed into the groom's, embodied the sacred act of entrusting her happiness to his care.

The application of sindoor, a crimson mark adorning the bride's forehead, and the draping of the auspicious mangalsutra around her neck, sealed their marital commitment, binding their souls in an unbreakable bond of love and devotion.

Each ceremony, a symphony of ancient rituals, infused the air with an aura of divine grace, weaving together the sacred threads that would form the tapestry of their union. From the sacred fire's radiant glow to the rhythmic beats of joyous celebrations, the wedding ceremonies resonated with the beauty and sanctity of a timeless tradition, painting a vivid tableau of love, unity, and cherished traditions.

Both the grooms and brides in separate Mandaps took all the vows. The main vows which they took were,

I will consider my wife to be my better half. I will look after her just as I look after myself.

I am accepting her as in-charge of my Home. I shall plan things in consultation with her.

I will never express dissatisfaction about any shortcomings in my wife.

I will always have faith in my wife. I will never look at another woman with the wrong intent.

I will be affectionate and treat my wife as a friend.

I will bring Home all the income to my wife.

I will not criticize my wife in front of others.

I will have a tolerant attitude towards my wife.

If my wife is unwell or unable to fulfill some

responsibilities. I will not withdraw support or refuse to fulfill my responsibilities towards her.

All these vows were committed for Kiran and Arya.

All the elders and the Pandit blessed them as under;

May these couples be blessed with an abundance of resources and comforts and be helpful to one another in all ways.

May these couples be strong and complement each other.

May these couples be blessed with property and riches.

May these couples be eternally happy.

May these couples be blessed with happy family life.

May these couples live in perfect harmony.

May these couples always be best of friends.

In separate Mandaps, both the grooms and the brides took vows, promising to consider each other as their better half, to plan things in consultation with each other, to never express dissatisfaction about any shortcomings in their spouse, and to always have faith and affection towards each other. The couple also vowed to bring all income home to their wives, to be tolerant towards each other, and to support each other even when unwell or unable to fulfill certain responsibilities.

After taking their vows, the elders and the Pandit

blessed the couples, wishing them an abundance of resources, comforts, and happiness, and hoping that they would complement each other, be blessed with property and riches, and live in perfect harmony, always being best of friends.

Finally, after all the ceremonies were performed, the couple became husband and wife, and a grand reception and dinner was held in the tastefully decorated open lawn of Ashoka Hotel. It was attended by the who's who of Delhi, Haryana, Western UP, and Rajasthan, making it a truly unforgettable night.

# 14

After a few days of marriage, Abhimanyu and Kiran planned to go to Nainital for their honeymoon. Kiran was nursing him to overcome his anxiety and symptoms of going for honeymoon. While Abhimanyu was struggling to fight his thought symptoms, Kiran was representing some powerful expression of reality. Kiran was more mature than Abhi and was always insisting and hesitantly explaining to him that honeymoon is not all about repeated sexual encounters but it is to understand and make both the people compatible.

ABHI: "Are you a Doctor or a Psychiatrist Kiran?"

KIRAN: "No, I am just your nurse to nurse all your problems and needs in life without even thinking twice. Please understand that I am a woman first, your girlfriend second, then a wife. I will keep you safe, well protected from all evils, dirty thoughts and other unwanted extra activities."

ABHI: "Arre, yaar, you are a magic pill in my life."

Abhimanyu described his experiences with an intensity that bordered on the divine. Every touch, every caress, every physical pleasure Kiran gave him felt like a gift from the heavens. Her touch was so essential to him that the mere thought of not feeling it made him fear for his life. Kiran, too, felt the same intense connection between them. As she sat against him, her hair tickling his face, Abhimanyu longed to absorb her completely, to meld their beings together. When Kiran confessed that his touch was like a fire that burned through her entire being, the two of them became twin points of a bright, white flame.

Abhi's wife felt his gaze and he opened one eye. She asked, "What are you doing?" Abhi replied, "Nothing." She asked, "What are you looking at me for?" Abhi said, "I wasn't looking... I was just thinking... Are you really going to be right there every night?" His wife responded with a simple "Yes" and an affirmative hum. Abhi was amazed and asked, "Forever?" His wife replied with a quiet "hmmm". Abhi then asked in disbelief, "You mean to say that of all the people in the world, the one to whom you will donate your naked-self night after night is me?" His wife affirmed, "Yes, I promised you that in one of our marriage vows." They then united in body and soul.

"Am I really that irresistible?" she asks, opening both eyes and urging Abhi to go back to sleep. The early morning nap was just too good to resist.

The next day, Abhi took Kiran for a boat ride in Naini Lake and they enjoyed the beauty of the green mountains surrounding the lake. After the boat ride, they went shopping on Mall Road when suddenly a hail storm and rain hit. In a short time, the entire road was covered with a white sheet of ice from the water and the weather became chilly but still enjoyable. They both had hot tea at a roadside tea stall.

Back at the hotel, the rooms were very cold, so Abhi asked for a room heater. With silk quilts and the heater, it became very cozy and they both felt a bit naughty. Abhi felt that Kiran was passionate, lusty, soft, and powerful - all at once. It was a mix of emotions that were enjoyed, appreciated, desired, feared, and confused. It was a part of the spiritual and biological aspects of their relationship.

KIRAN - "Abhi, seeing you so happy is the happiest and proudest moment for me."

ABHI - "I always knew that I had married a woman with a stunning beauty and an even more beautiful heart and mind."

After their ten-day honeymoon, they returned home and were warmly welcomed by Abhi's parents.

# 15

Abhinandan and Arya returned home after an extravagant honeymoon that lasted one month. They visited many beautiful places around the world, including Las Vegas, England, France, Paris, Belgium, Amsterdam, Munich, Innobruca, Italy, Venice, Florence, Rome, Pisa, Valenza, Lucerne, Mt. Titlis, Jungfraujoch, and Geneva. Abhinandan had carefully planned the honeymoon and chose Las Vegas as their first destination. Las Vegas is a magical place for a honeymoon, where one can experience fun, excitement, and endless possibilities. They stayed at the Four Seasons Hotel, where they also rented a cabana and spent the day by the pool. In the evening, they took a yoga class beside the dolphins at the Secret

Garden and Dolphin Habitat in the Mirage Hotel. They explored the city and visited famous hotels like The Bellagio, The Venetian, Red Rock Casino Resort and Spa, and The Mirage Hotel. The temperature was pleasant, around 25°C, and they enjoyed their dinner at a roadside food joint.

Abhinandan and Arya had an intimate and passionate relationship, where they could communicate their likes and dislikes without hesitation. They were inseparable, even in bed, where they could enjoy each other without fear of performance or pregnancy. Their lovemaking produced a spiritual fusion that strengthened their bond. The next day, they enjoyed a helicopter ride over the Grand Canyon and saw the city from a bird's eye view.

Arya shared with Abhinandan that her favorite part of their European trip was their excursion to Jungfraujoch, the top of Europe, where they saw snow-clad mountains and went ice skating. She also enjoyed the bus ride throughout Europe, which was a wonderful experience she would never forget. Abhinandan was happy to hear that but knew that the best part of their honeymoon was being with each other. They finally returned to Rohtak after a month of adventure and love.

# 16

As Abhimanyu boarded the military jeep, he cast one final look at Kiran who stood at the gate, her back turned to him. It was his first deployment since their marriage, and the emotions were palpable. The gravity of the situation was not lost on either of them. Abhimanyu was headed to Machil sector in Jammu and Kashmir, a place known for dense forests and terror infestation, supported by none other than the Pakistan army.

Despite the heart-wrenching goodbye, Kiran held her emotions in check. She knew the importance of staying strong for her husband and her family. For her, Abhimanyu was a hero with superhuman abilities, the backbone of the entire army system. She understood that being an army wife meant standing tall and supporting her family, no matter the emotional turbulence.

As the jeep disappeared from view, Kiran couldn't help but think about the incredible strength and courage Abhimanyu possessed. She knew that he was first and foremost a soldier, but also a loving husband. She whispered to herself, "Together for always and never apart, maybe in distance but never in heart."

Kiran took a deep breath and promised to be as brave as her husband. She knew that she was the power behind POWER. She would manage everything on her own, and never let her emotions get the better of her. For Kiran, a positive attitude was everything, despite the ongoing concerns and worries.

As Abhimanyu set foot on the path of his noble mission, Kiran clung to the unwavering belief that their separation would be temporary, and their reunion would be a testament to their unwavering love and indomitable spirit. With every passing day, her heart whispered promises of their eventual embrace, filled with the conviction that their bond would emerge even stronger and more resilient than ever before.

Yet, for the time being, Kiran found solace in the strength she derived from being a pillar of support for her beloved family. Just as Abhimanyu drew courage from his duty to protect and serve his nation, she, too, had to summon her inner fortitude to stand tall amidst the challenges that confronted her.

With unwavering determination, Kiran navigated the ebbs and flows of daily life, shouldering responsibilities with grace and resilience. She became the rock upon which her family leaned, offering solace and support, embodying the unwavering strength that mirrored her husband's dedication to his nation.

Though their physical presence may be separated by miles and adversity, the unbreakable bond they shared remained a source of inspiration, fueling their resolve to overcome any obstacle that crossed their path. Kiran's unwavering faith in their love and shared destiny kept her anchored, assuring her that their paths would converge once again, intertwining their lives in a beautiful tapestry of love, strength, and resilience.

As the days turned into weeks and the weeks into months, Kiran's unwavering spirit shone brightly, a beacon of hope that illuminated her family's path. She drew strength from the love they shared, knowing that their unwavering support for one another would carry them through the trials they faced.

With each passing day, Kiran's love for Abhimanyu grew deeper, nurturing the flame of their connection and fueling her determination to remain strong until the day they would reunite. In her heart, she held the belief that their love transcended physical distance and time, weaving a bond that would withstand any adversity.

Thus, as Abhimanyu embarked on his noble mission, Kiran carried the weight of their love and hope upon her shoulders. With unwavering faith, she embraced her role as a source of strength for her family, embodying the resilience and unwavering spirit that mirrored her husband's dedication to his duty.

Together, they stood as pillars of strength, united by a love that defied all odds, patiently awaiting the moment when their paths would converge once again, and their love would flourish anew, stronger and more resilient than ever before.

# 17

Time flew by. While her husband, Abhimanyu Singh, was away serving on the J&K border, Kiran found herself with some free time to pursue something she had long been passionate about: research. She had already completed her PhD in Hindi Literature and now she set her sights on a D.Litt, a degree awarded for exceptional research in literature, administration, and social sciences. Pursuing a career in research was daunting and highly competitive, but Kiran was ready for the challenge.

She carefully crafted her research thesis on "UTTAR KAND," a literary work by Valmiki, and estimated the time and effort required to complete the project. As a senior researcher, Kiran knew the importance of networking, learning, and seizing future opportunities. To achieve her goals, she knew she needed courage, persistence, and the ability to ask the right questions and seek guidance from her peers and experts.

Kiran understood that challenges were inevitable on the road to success, but she refused to let them deter her. She believed that resilience in the face of adversity was the key to success. With this mindset, she sought out mentors to guide and support her at each stage of her research journey. Finding the right mentor who understood her aspirations and provided the necessary support became crucial to Kiran's success.

Through hard work, determination, and unwavering self-belief, Kiran was on her way to achieving her goals as a successful researcher.

She made some self-discovery questions like;

1) What are you trying to achieve in the next 5 years?
2) What are your strengths and weaknesses?
3) Which strength would you like to cultivate in the upcoming years?
4) What happens when things don't work?
5) How can you keep yourselves motivated?
6) How do you connect with your team?
7) How can you add value to your institution with your research?

She made these questions printed on cardboard

and was seeing them everyday. Kiran was intelligent, very logical, a good wife, a good daughter and a good daughter in-law. The only point of debate in her life was to follow all right things except becoming a KOWTOW, which means extraordinary reverence for her father which was like a deep respect to her father even if the father is not justified in asking anything to do.

"I WILL NEVER EVER ARGUE WITH MY FATHER COME WHAT MAY" was the motto of her life.

# 18

As the old adage goes, time and tide wait for none. Abhimanyu found himself posted in the turbulent region of Jammu and Kashmir, while Abhinandan and Arya had been married for almost eight months now.

Pregnancy is a challenging and overwhelming phase of a woman's life. During this time, a woman needs all the love, care, and support she can get. When blessed with a caring mother-in-law, handling pregnancy becomes a tad bit easier. Such a mother-in-law ensures that her daughter-in-law gets everything she needs, from a healthy diet to a sound sleep. In fact, pregnancy can be the time when the bond between the two women strengthens quite a lot. However, Kirti Singh's dreams and expectations came crashing down like a pack of cards when she learned that Arya had not yet conceived. Disappointment was an inevitable part of life that surfaced when hopes or expectations were not met. Kirti Singh, after tolerating and riding the wave of disappointment, preferred to talk to Arya and Abhinandan Singh, expressing her emotions.

Arya's in-laws especially Kirti Singh were getting impatient everyday for Arya not conceiving and according to her belief that there is a biological clock ticking for grandparents too. Their constant nagging was not helping Arya to reproduce. In the initial stages after marriage both Abhinandan and Arya were taking a shelter under the disguise of family planning. Arya was telling her mother in-law Kirti Singh that your son only doesn't want a baby now but in-laws often have definite reasons for sticking their noses for reasons like;

1) They want to see their bloodline continue.
2) They yearn to have the family name passed down through the generations.
3) They have built something, they value such as family Farming and they want to keep it in the family.
4) They feel that by not having children, you are deviating from normal behavior as per society.
5) They want their grandchildren to keep them busy and entertained.

6) They genuinely enjoy raising kids.

Both Abhinandan and Arya appreciated their in-laws' concern, as they likely had their best interests at heart. However, managing her opinionated in-laws proved difficult for Arya, as she couldn't afford to start a war with them. Instead, she remained calm and tactful. When the pressure from Kirti Singh became too much, Arya assured her that she appreciated their concern and would definitely heed their advice. She even hinted at consulting an established gynecologist soon.

While sex is a sacred subject, Arya felt it necessary to take her mother-in-law into confidence, despite constant interference making both her and Abhinandan irritated and disappointed. They never blamed each other, acknowledging that it was taking longer than expected to get pregnant, and disappointment was a natural feeling. Building a family and parenting were fundamental parts of life, and when they didn't come easily, it could make them feel as if something was wrong with them. Abhinandan and Arya realized they had some ups and downs towards getting pregnant.

So, they decided to consult an infertility specialist and fixed an appointment with them. The specialist told them that many problems are relatively easy to treat, and getting diagnosed could spare them a lot of further disappointment.

# 19

Abhimanyu called up his father Col. Ranjit Singh. He seemed concerned about the border tension and Pakistan Army's repeated attempts to push the local terrorists trained across the border and foreign terror groups but he said, it could not be discussed as it is a sensitive subject. He also advised his father not to worry that the situation on the ground is not like it is being made out in Media. Col. Ranjit Singh said, "I am both concerned and proud. I always wanted your son to join the Indian Army. I know son that you are a man of steel, standing tall in the harshest of conditions. You have always disregarded freezing cold temperatures and scorching heat to remain brave, awake and devoted to our country and then to us."

Remember Abhi that I have been an Indian Army officer who lived a life of adventure and Heroism, grappling with the Nation's enemies in the freezing Himalayas or the burning deserts of Rajasthan. Your job would be to fight to win. Be careful but if the situation warrants, face the bullet on the chest and not on the back. I am proud of you Abhi and we all love you including the iron lady called your wife, your soulmate.

"I am proud of you Dad, you would always find your son above average of all your expectations. My heart swells with pride when I talk to you, Col. Singh."

Please tell Kiran that I will speak to her in the evening. Hopefully the situation on the ground would improve.

The guns were silent from both Indian and Pakistan troops in the Machil sector across the line of control. The meeting between foreign ministers of both the countries was going on in New Delhi. Abhimanyu apart from being a fierce soldier, was a core romantic person but now, he was more responsible, punctual and sincere for both his army duties and his love for Kiran unlike the time before meeting Kiran. He called up Kiran;

"I watched as Kiran's face lit up with joy, her thoughts clearly lost in the moment. 'If you love an army officer, raise your glass and if any army officer loves you then raise your head and walk like a queen,' she repeated a statement by Queen Elizabeth. 'I am actually walking like a queen,' she told me with a wide grin.

I couldn't help but feel a surge of happiness at the sight of her excitement. 'Kiran, if things go well, I might meet you next month,' I said, 'and I am expecting you to be called Ma'am by me and every friend of mine whosoever he expects to meet. I know you are working hard to adopt army things but adaptability actually was working way too hard for you.'

Kiran nodded, a determined expression on her face. 'To be a wife of an army officer you have to possess a lot of perseverance with an equal amount of optimism and adaptability,' she replied. 'I had to garner faith and courage to be a true companion of an army officer like you. I always feel proud when I watch you in uniform.'

'Yes, really?' I asked, a hint of doubt in my voice.

Kiran's eyes shone with sincerity. 'Abhi, there is no denying that love can do wonders on you whether you're head over heels or completely swept away.'

'Yes, Kiran, when it comes to love, dopamine isn't the only chemical but oxytocin levels also surge,' I said, wanting to impress her with my knowledge. 'That's why you probably feel comfortable and relaxed.'

Kiran laughed, the sound musical and light. 'Have you gone to the J & K border to fight the enemies or learn and teach love effects?' she teased. 'Do you have some female friends around or what?'

I shook my head, a smirk playing at the corners of my lips. 'There is no trace of females up to miles and miles,' I replied, before turning to watch the sunset together with Kiran, my heart filled with love and contentment."

Kiran stares at Sky, watches the stars and thinks the beginning of love, the falling in love, gave her the starry wet eyes and butterflies in the stomach.

The phone gets disconnected.

# 20

The fact that Arya was unable to conceive was putting a strain on two relationships in her life – those with her husband and mother-in-law. As time went on, her relationships with both Abhinandan Singh and Kirti Singh deteriorated, causing concern for the entire family. As her chances of fertility decreased and her stress levels rose, Arya became vulnerable to taunts from family, friends, and society. However, she knew that this journey was one that she and Abhinandan needed to face together.

Virendra Singh, Arya's father-in-law, advised his wife to be mindful of her daughter-in-law's vulnerabilities and not to hurt her further. A wise member of their family suggested that Abhinandan should also share responsibility for their situation rather than blaming Arya alone.

In an effort to identify the root of the problem, Abhinandan and Arya sought medical aid through detailed diagnosis and treatment. Abhinandan underwent semen analysis and blood tests to evaluate his hormone levels and genetic testing to rule out any genetic defects. The doctor confirmed that his test results were satisfactory and within acceptable parameters.

Arya underwent specific fertility tests, including ovulation tests, Hysterosalpingography to evaluate the condition of her uterus and fallopian tubes, and ovarian reserve testing to determine the quantity of eggs. Imaging tests, pelvic ultrasounds, and sonohysterograms were also conducted to identify any potential uterine disease. Hysteroscopy and laparoscopy were performed to pinpoint the specific problem.

Unfortunately, the compiled test results were disheartening and horrifying. The doctors confirmed that any further treatments may be ineffective, and there was no guarantee that any treatment would work. Some causes, such as genetic conditions or inoperable scarring of the reproductive organs, could mean that infertility is permanent. The news was devastating for everyone, especially Arya and Abhinandan. The disappointment increased the risk of physical and emotional difficulties, such as headaches, stomach problems, and excessive perspiration.

The worst mental agony Arya faced was a comment from her own mother in-law "Well after Arya's IVF failed, her mother-in-law came out of the room and told Arya it's OVER NOW so focus on household work." Arya became a sort of nervous breakdown patient. She started "I don't understand why we must do things in this world, why we must have friends and aspirations, hopes and dreams. We would lose everything and gain nothing, for what is there to be gained from this world?"

"As far as I am concerned, I resign from humanity. I no longer want to be nor can I still be a woman? Hunt for the weakness in these philosophical systems, fight for moral and esthetic ideals? I hate wise men, they are cowardly and prudent. People just get pleasure from others' pain. I can not contribute anything to this world because I only have one thing with me, AGONY."

Abhinandan and Kiran were the only acceptable support system for Arya. Arya could simply look for the silver lining in her situation. She could think hard enough. Finding these good things to focus, helped her overcome feelings of disappointment.

Another Silver lining for Arya was that she was able to adjust her feelings by broadening her thinking. The broadening of thinking happened to Kirti Singh also but Kirti Singh could never forgo her intense desire of having grandchildren for continuity of their family lineage. Though it was a load of narcissistic nonsense because firstly she won't be able to see the name after she is dead and secondly what's so important about her family name? Most importantly if the Child is a girl, would it mean the end of her family name?

But nothing could alter the mindset of Arya's mother-in-law, Mrs.Kirti Singh.

# 21

On J&K borders, positive development was taking place for the last 48 hours and the diplomatic sources of the Indian Government informed the forces and they welcomed the denial of a war ultimatum. Pakistan's foreign minister requested to relocate the Indian forces to a peacetime location. Indian Army headed by Major Abhimanyu Singh denied that there was a build-up of troops on the border and confirmed that the troops are only on alert. It was only Pakistan that whipped up war rhetoric. Pakistan said that it would positively take action against terrorists found involved in the terrorism.

Guns were silent on both Indian and Pakistan sides in the Machil sector across the Line of Control and the tension and stress on both sides' troops was reduced.

Abhimanyu would always come up with his ways of surprising Kiran and would always keep the conversation lively as he would have many stories to tell about his encounters with the enemies and terrorists. Kiran was feeling lucky as there was a call and text messages at least once a day saying "I am Okay, Love you baby". These calls and messages were melting Kiran's heart and kept her going for an eternity. They both started counting days when they would be back together.

Abhi nervously dialed Kiran's number, waiting for her to pick up. When she finally did, his heart leapt in his chest. "How are you baby?" he asked, his voice full of longing.

"I am good, counting and cutting lines each day for your arrival," Kiran replied, her voice soft and tender.

Abhi couldn't help but smile at her words. "There is no pleasure bigger than waiting to meet you," he said.

Kiran's voice suddenly grew serious. "I have something important to discuss with you actually in person but immediately it is not possible for you," she said.

Abhi felt his anxiety rise. "Tell me baby but before I know the details tell me first what are you doing and what are you wearing?" he asked, trying to distract himself.

"Just taking a shower and drying my tresses," Kiran said.

"With wet hair on your shoulder, you must be looking like a temptation for me to have a look at you. Now tell me what you are wearing or planning to wear?" Abhi asked, unable to resist teasing her.

Kiran laughed lightly. "I am in a casual outfit white top and light blue jeans with light makeup. You seem to be not interested in listening to my important discussion?" she said.

Abhi suddenly heard gunshots in the background, and his heart skipped a beat. "I am sorry Kiran, there was some noise of gun fires. Please go ahead," he said, his voice tense.

"Yes, I wanted to say that to you for so long," Kiran began, her voice shaking slightly. "I can't think of anything other than you with me to have you more and more and spend the rest of my moments with you."

Abhi felt a lump form in his throat. "Kiran, it's the same here. How do I make you believe that I love you to the moon and back and now that a piece of my heart is always missing you when you are not with me. The feeling of inadequacy is running so deep within me that I don't want to be termed as a selfish lover," he said, his voice full of emotion.

"Abhi, be careful there and under the circumstances,

I do not want you to venture outside," Kiran warned him. "I don't want your life to be jeopardized. There are many beautiful girls in the valley and also during your encounters, just do not go astray towards HUNZA valley of Pakistan. HUNZA has the most beautiful females in the world."

"On this earth there is no one as beautiful as you Baby," Abhi assured her. "You are my Miss India, you are my Miss Universe. Good relationships never ask for explanations because there is a silent understanding and a deep faith of unconditional love and trust existing in each other's life."

Kiran suddenly changed the subject, her voice heavy with concern. "Arya has undergone all the medical tests for conceiving a child. She is facing a lot of misery and disappointment," she said.

"I feel sorry for both Arya and Abhinandan. I'll speak to them, especially Arya, shortly," Abhi promised, his mind racing with thoughts of his loved ones.

Immediately after the call ended, Abhimanyu Singh was urgently deputed on the hardline front at Pampore which Kiran was not aware of.

# 22

Abhimanyu reported to Lt. Col Krishnamurthy at Pampore front where he commanded the people and resources available with him that he deemed necessary for a particular situation. The situation at the Pampore front was very volatile and very dangerous. Under pressure, under stress he initially took charge of repairs, maintenance and inspection of army equipment, participating in production and quality control of spare parts and acting as a liaison with his commanding officer and headquarters at Delhi.

He was assisted by 10 Parachute Regiment and strong troops of Jat Regiment. He was part of two successful operations in which four terrorists were eliminated. Abhimanyu was adjudged as a dynamic officer and a true commando.

Guerillas believed to be foreigners from Pakistan and Afghanistan sneaked into the army camp after cutting through two layered barbed wire at 4:30AM. The attackers first hurled grenades and started firing indiscriminately causing casualties to three Indian Soldiers. The army led by Major Abhimanyu Singh retaliated and killed two intruders and the third intruder escaped taking advantage of darkness.

Major Abhimanyu Singh got minor injuries in the massive encounter and was advised to go on sick leave but he declined and offered to continue fighting the insurgency in the valley. Kiran was informed as if it was just a minor accident but she was all aware of the hardships officers in the defense forces had to face. She never expressed but lived in constant fear specially sometimes waiting for days to get a call from Abhi informing her that he is Okay. It is tough and it was really tough but it puts so many other things in perspective. Inspite knowing Abhi's injury, she always appreciated Abhimanyu's passion towards his country and his uniform.

The realities of his service were complex and rarely romantic. His life was a lot tough and Kiran could never explain because it could only be experienced. The life of Major Abhimanyu Singh sometimes was frustrating.

The only solace he had, was some romantic exchange with Kiran, yes their love life was eternal and their long distance relationship passed all the tests of time and the hope of meeting soon, kept both of them strong here and there. Their unexpected calls every now and then made their days.

The most important lesson which Kiran learnt from Abhi was humility. She was managing the house like both son and daughter in-law. Even if she wanted to crib eloquently about her problems to her faraway and injured husband. On the phone, she never did it because he felt that he shouldn't be bogged down by her worries. He needed peace of mind to do his duties well, amid difficulties and danger. She always knew that Abhi is a soldier first and a husband only next but still there was always the fear looming at the back of her mind over her husband's safety. There was this inevitable long wait for his safe return which actually was her test of patience.

Kiran has learned to live in any kind of situation that life in the Army throws at her and behind every strong soldier like Abhi, there is an even stronger braveheart who is the Army wife- Kiran.

# 23

Abhi came Home on leave after spending a very successful hard life with no injury. Only a scar on my right leg. Kiran was on Cloud 9. She was in fact waiting and needing her prince charming and was in full mood of love and romance from head to toe. Loving an army officer comes with consequences. It is just not easy but loving that one hero in combat boots is worth every pain, every lonely night and every single second without him. When Abhi returned back and held Kiran into his arms, she fell prey to every touch, caress, kiss, every word. She memorized the feel of his skin, his smell, the sound of his voice and played it over and over. It was never enough to love him and hold him and yet it was always tough to let him go. It was never easy to deal with the constant absence of my army husband, always on duty mode, no Saturdays, no Sundays, no Calendar Holidays even.

When Abhimanyu was at Home, their life was also about fun, parties, socializing and a lot of glamor. As Kiran was very fond of Chocolates and Roses, Abhi arranged without losing even one hour. Abhi remembered that on his last visit Kiran had her heart set on a particular article of Jewelry. He did get it for her this time. Both Kiran and Abhi celebrated Valentine day with great enthusiasm and for the first time, he took his wife for a ballroom dance and woman of the Indian Forces award in Navy Nagar and celebrated Kiran being awarded the woman of substance.

Next week, they met Arya and explained to her not to get disappointed as she is not the only woman who has such issues. It is never necessary for every mother to have her biological child. You could adopt one and help the destitute child to get a mother. I am your brother-in-law so I can flirt around with you and I will give you one of Kiran's children. The choice would be yours whether you opt for a son or daughter. I will also talk to Abhinandan and your mother in-law when Abhinandan returns from the court.

On the week-end Abhinandan planned a tour of Rajasthan. Abhinandan, Arya, Abhimanyu, Kiran and

Abhinandan's parents were all excited. Abhinandan made this plan to raise Arya's spirits and to bring her out of despair. He explained to the entire group that the Indian State of Rajasthan is popularly known to many as the land of Kings, is a beautiful example of Indian age-old opulence and grandeur. Rajasthan is one of the most colorful and vibrant States with a strong blend of culture, history, music, cuisine, falling in love with Rajasthan doesn't take much time.

Abhinandan took a nine night, ten days package tour. This tour package covered major tourist destinations of Rajasthan which included the visit to Jaipur, Shekhawati, Ranakpur, Fatehpur, Jaisalmer, Jodhpur, Bikaner, Mount Abu, Udaipur, Ajmer and Pushkar. They had the opportunity to visit the monuments and know about the culture and rich heritage of the State. Both Kiran and Arya enjoyed the elephant ride of Amer Fort and dinner at Chokhi Dhani in Jaipur. Arya being with her sister Kiran also relished the experience of the boat ride in beautiful lake Pichola at Udaipur. They all enjoyed the Camel ride and dinner over the dunes at Jaisalmer.

The basic purpose of Abhimanyu and Kiran was to bring back life to both Arya and Abhinandan Singh. Arya returned Home with no disappointment and cordial relations with her mother in-law.

## 24

After a month a dreadful day came when Abhimanyu was to resume his army duty that too his third posting in hard area Shopian which is considered a hotbed of engagements between militants and the security forces.

It was one of the toughest things to say goodbye to Abhimanyu. The feeling of sadness seems to overwhelm all. Just the thought of Abhi leaving home causes heartache. It was more difficult for Kiran as without him this home will feel so empty. Kiran said to Abhi "Genuinely your smile radiated and spread a ray of positivity. When you laugh, you make sure that everyone laughs with you. You care for us like your own being and we all became a family". Arya is a living example. Arya said, "your presence makes a lot of difference in our lives. It is inevitable to admit that you are definitely the most loved and adored person in the family. Your smile not only lights up the room but also hearts. What I and Kiran will miss about you is that you greet everyone. Something is just very distinct about you. Your vibes that you radiate are positive and glowing. Your energy is unmatchable and your absence in this house will make us miss you. You are the purest of all humans. You are honest, genuine and generous. Finally before leaving the gate Kiran said, "My man, my soldier being a fierce soldier is a core romantic person, a responsible husband, I will miss you Abhi."

Abhimanyu left to be on the border in Shopian near LOC with Pakistan.

The moment Kiran saw Abhi's back beyond the main gate of her house she went in a pensive mood, I never thought, this day would come, I mean I did know, it was coming but I just never thought it would be this soon." As a tremendous storm, an urge of crying overwhelmed Kiran and all she could do was to sit down, hide her face in her hands and let her emotions overpower her. She cried like a baby but Abhimanyu had gone so far.

# 25

In the Shopian sector across the Line of Control, there was an eerie silence from both Indian and Pakistan troops as the foreign ministers of both countries met in New Delhi for peace talks. However, the Pakistan army attempted to infiltrate a heavily armed group of militants into Kashmir from across the LOC.

Upon learning of this, Col. Baljit Singh Sandhu summoned Major Abhimanyu Singh, a seasoned officer who was familiar with the area, to lead a battalion of Jat Regiment. Abhimanyu's task was to eliminate the militants and send a strong message of retaliation to the Pakistan army.

Abhimanyu wasted no time and took charge of the area that same night. He and his team conducted intensive patrolling and night searches, locating the entry points where the militants were planning to enter under cover fire from the Pakistan Army. A fierce gun battle ensued, leaving 15 militants dead and one Junior Commissioned Officer (JCO) of the Indian Army dead.

Despite this success, Abhimanyu was warned to maintain the same position as there were 35 terror camps operational in Pakistan-occupied Kashmir and close to 200 militants were waiting to cross over to J&K. Using intelligence gathered by his team, Abhimanyu successfully foiled six infiltration bids on his side of the LOC.

Meanwhile, diplomatic discussions between India and Pakistan continued, but the ground realities were far from peaceful. Threats to vital installations and the economy were increasing, prompting the Indian Army to move towards the India-Pakistan border. Villages close to the border were evacuated and arrangements were made to settle the displaced people in religious places.

Abhimanyu was in charge of the most critical areas, and there was a heavy build-up of the Pakistan Army in Machhiwara where he was stationed. A sixteen-hour fierce fight ensued, with the Indian Army launching a counterattack near an abandoned house where a team of Pakistan snipers were holed up. Abhimanyu's team cordoned off the area and a major gunfight broke out, resulting in the death of the entire elite team of Pakistan Army.

Despite being outnumbered by Pakistan tanks and other military inventory, Abhimanyu's bravery led India to victory. His regiment decided to put up a brave front, and he inspired his team to march forward and meet the enemy at 3 Kms inside Pakistan territory. Though Abhimanyu was injured and his tank was on fire, he refused to retreat and continued firing until all the enemy tanks were destroyed.

In the end, Abhimanyu was badly injured and profusely bleeding. However, his core team picked him up and rushed him to an army medical camp and then to an army hospital in Amritsar for proper treatment.

# 26

Major Abhimanyu was given primary medical help for injuries at army base camp but he had to be shifted immediately to Military hospital, Amritsar for his grievous injuries. According to the medical report his condition was said to be stable. However the armed forces Doctors and medics were prepared for the worst scenario. They were trained to deal with trauma and injuries as a normal part of their service.

An expert panel of Military Doctors and Specialists drawn from private hospitals like All India Institute of Medical Science AIIMS NEW DELHI, P.G.I. Chandigarh, Dr.Shetty from Bengaluru were called to provide medication to Major Abhimanyu Singh. After conducting X-Ray, ECG, ECHO tests, they clarified that there was no permanent damage to his organs and limbs but Dr.Shekhar Krishan had his reservations to clear him from SPINAL CORD INJURY (SCI) and needed some more tests. According to him, there were certain symptoms of damage of Spinal Cord that could cause changes in its function either temporary or permanent. These changes later might translate into loss of muscle function, sensation or autonomic function in parts of the body served by the spinal cord below the level of the lesion. Abhimanyu was constantly complaining of extreme back pain, weakness, numbness and tingling sensation in hands, feet and fingers.

Kiran was called to see her husband. She was informed about injuries of Abhimanyu only after he was brought to Military Hospital, Amritsar. She came with her father in-law Col. Ranjit Singh and her mother Rajbala Singh.

Kiran was not out of trauma and anxiety tending towards depression and turmoil. She was expecting the unexpected. Though Kiran being the wife of an army officer and daughter in-law of a very senior army officer belonged to a special breed. She was an extraordinary wife and was in love with a soldier who might not return after having gone to a heavy war zone at LOC.

Seeing her husband in hospital in helpless

conditions, she broke down and started crying loudly like a baby but as an army wife was not supposed to weep. Col. Ranjit Singh took her away from the hospital wards. Dr.Krishnan asked her to sign certain documents as a basic requirement of the hospital before he could proceed with the surgical operation to rectify the injury to the Spinal Cord. Surgery to treat Spinal Cord Injury (SCI), was performed immediately. The operation lasted for nine long hours and Abhimanyu was shifted to ICU with strict instructions not to allow anyone to be close to him, except medics for next 48 hours. Dr.Krishnan informed Kiran and Col. Ranjit Singh that the operation had been done. Major Abhimanyu's all body functions would work normally including his neuro system except he would need a walker support all the time. He would not be able to move independently and would need a constant watch from the family.

Kiran was advised to take extra care to keep him maintaining his moral spirits high and needed to do more than being just the spouse. Kiran understood the gravity of the situation and assured the Doctor that she would do much more than being just the spouse, Maybe she would be a Sister (Nurse) in addition to being his wife.

Kiran also informed her mother in-law Mrs.

Veermati Singh about the details of Abhi's injuries and medication in Military Hospital, Amritsar.

Major Abhimanyu's mother arrived the next day and had the shock of her life when she learnt the truth of her gallant and brave son but nearly fainted when she saw Abhimanyu. She was deeply pained as her pain of seeing her son in these conditions was the biggest of her life. Seeing Mrs.Veermati so shattered and pathetic, Col. Ranjit Singh pacified her saying that no one should be held responsible for Abhimanyu's condition as it was his own Karma.

Major Abhimanyu Singh was unconscious all these days and was being monitored on hourly basis by the medics. There was no sign of improvement except hope. He was unable to respond to people and activities around. After three days Abhimanyu's eyes were wide open but brain was shut. All the people of the family present in the hospital were called and were advised by the Doctors to talk to him irrespective of whether he responds or doesn't because according to them, such unconscious persons may benefit from the familiar voices of loved ones which may help awaken the unconscious brain and speed up recovery. Everyone spoke to him.

Abhi lay in his hospital bed, his body battered and broken from the battle he had just fought. As he opened his eyes, he saw Kiran standing by his side, her voice like music to his ears. "How are you feeling baby?" she asked, her hand reaching out to touch his.

Abhi caught Kiran's hand tightly and tears started rolling down his cheeks. "I will miss you," he whispered, his voice choked with emotion. Kiran wiped his tears, her heart heavy with the weight of his pain.

"You are a Soldier first, then the lover only next," she reminded him gently. "You are a divine gift to me, and everything you have done has strengthened me. Be strong. Life will always test you, and you have to fight back and not give up. It is always dark before dawn."

Abhi listened to her words, drawing strength from her love and support. "Every day, when I wake up in the morning, I am filled with gratitude that I have another life to love and enjoy every moment with you," he said, his voice filled with determination.

Even in his comatose state, Abhi knew that Kiran was his reason to keep fighting, to keep pushing through the darkness and into the light. With her by his side, he knew he could overcome any obstacle and emerge stronger than ever before.

After a while, Abhimanyu suffered sudden bouts of convulsions. The nurse came out running and updated the Doctors about Abhi's conditions. He was shifted to the Operation Theatre.

Major Abhimanyu Singh was surrounded by a multidisciplinary team consisting of Surgeons, Physicians, Nurses and Rehabilitation Specialists. The heart surgery was done and he was also injected with anti seizure medicine to control possible seizures. In the Operation Theatre, Abhimanyu again suffered sudden bouts of convulsions. He was moving towards Coma. The Doctors tried their best to help Abhimanyu to get out of Coma. Abhimanyu experienced a stroke and a blood clot blocked the blood supply to parts of his brain. His brain was completely damaged. The Doctors tried all means to revive his life. They did their best but the final cardiac arrest took away Abhimanyu's life.

Dr. Shetty came out of O.T. and with a sad expression informed Col. Ranjit Singh, Mrs.Veermati Singh and Kiran that Abhimanyu was no more. They have failed to save him.

As the heart-wrenching news of Abhi's untimely demise reached Kiran's ears, her world crumbled beneath her feet. The weight of grief bore down on her like an unbearable burden, causing her fragile body to succumb to the overwhelming anguish. Overwhelmed by the sudden loss of their beloved son, her parents were thrust into a tumultuous sea of sorrow, their very souls shattered by the painful reality that now engulfed them.

In the wake of such a devastating incident, the rawness of their emotions was laid bare, leaving them with a profound sense of helplessness and despair. Tears flowed ceaselessly, their sorrow intermingling as they sought solace in one another's arms, desperately trying to find a semblance of comfort in their shared grief.

As they clung to each other, memories of Abhimanyu's radiant smile and infectious laughter flickered through their minds like bittersweet snapshots frozen in time. Each recollection carried a poignant reminder of the joy he had once brought to their lives, now hauntingly absent. The heaviness in Kiran's heart deepened, casting a shadow of desolation upon her soul, as she grappled with the unbearable void left by his departure.

In the midst of their profound anguish, Kiran's spirit felt fragmented and lost, aching with a profound sense of dejection. The world around her seemed to fade into insignificance as she mourned the loss of a life so full of promise and potential. Each beat of her heart was laced with a profound longing for the return of the vibrant soul that had been snatched away so abruptly.

Thus, in the wake of Abhi's devastating departure, Kiran and her parents found themselves entwined in a tapestry of grief and resilience. Their hearts shattered, but not broken, they clung to the remnants of love and cherished memories, forging a path through the depths of despair, fueled by the indomitable spirit of their beloved Abhimanyu.

# 27

Abhimanyu's body was draped in a White cloth and National Flag in a Casket and was kept in the hall of Military Hospital in Amritsar. Abhimanyu's mother fainted again after seeing her son's lifeless body. The body was surrounded by family members.

When Abhimanyu's mother Veermati Singh regained consciousness, she saw a big group of Doctors and senior Army officers. Chief of the army staff General Kumar was also present there. He briefed Col. Ranjit Singh, Veermati Singh, Kiran and all the family members of Major Abhimanyu Singh about the glorious fight of Maj. Abhimanyu Singh said, "It's because of Major Abhimanyu Singh's solo efforts and courage, we have been able to defend the sovereignty of our borders and we as a nation would ever remain indebted to his exemplary service to India.

The army brass further added that Abhimanyu's deeds to protect Mother India would not remain a news item so routinely read and forgotten but that would remind the entire young officers of Indian Army to imitate. Thank you Mrs.Veermati Singh and Col. Ranjit Singh for such a wonderful service of your son to the Indian Army. We owe a deep debt of gratitude to officers like Major Abhimanyu Singh. We also express our grief and gratitude to Mrs.Kiran Singh who stood like a rock from his war days to his medication days in Military Hospital, Amritsar. Indian Army would always remain indebted to you, your brave son and your responsible daughter in-law. JAY HIND.

Kiran's face resplendent with pride in being the wife of such a brave soldier though she was controlling with difficulty not to burst into tears and express her deadly disappointment.

Kiran said, "I am thankful for the kindness and generosity shown to me and my family. Words can not express our gratitude and appreciation for such a wonderful caring community called INDIAN ARMY. Abhimanyu is not there with us, but I am sure if I had a son, I would have also made him a better Soldier, the worthy son of a worthy father. I thank you all for everything you have done for Major Abhimanyu Singh, my husband, JAY HIND.

The mortal remains of Major Abhimanyu Singh who was martyred in the line of duty two days back while fighting infiltrators and the Pakistan army reached Rohtak city at 8:30PM yesterday. The Casket was brought home today at 7:00AM. Abhimanyu wasn't there, yet she couldn't accept or would ever accept that he was dead and would not come back to take care of her and the family. Kiran couldn't control her tears and asked, "Abhi, you promised me that you would never leave me, what happened to your promise? You know that I can't live without you." Col. Ranjit Singh consoled her, "Kiran you are strength in yourself. Tears gusted from the eyes of both Kiran and her father in-law. Kiran left the drawing room as she couldn't take it any more. She had too many regrets.

Among the people who came for condolence, the family happened to have quite a learned man from ISKCON Temple that happened absolutely unplanned and unprepared. She saw Kiran weeping continuously and repeatedly murmuring , "Why me?" She asked Kiran to surrender to Lord Krishna. I am sorry for your grief but you are not the only woman who has faced such tragedy. He quoted some excerpts from Mahabharata. The content of my explanation is pretty large but I will give you a brief description for your own consumption.

In Mahabharata, Karna expressed his tragedies like;

1) My mother left me the moment I was born. Is it my fault to be born as an illegitimate child?
2) I didn't get an education from Dronacharya. I was not considered a Kshatriya.
3) Parsuram taught me but then gave me a curse to forget everything when he came to know that I was the son of Kunti.
4) I was disgraced in Draupadi's Swayamvar.
5) Whatever I received was through Duryodhan's charity.

Krishna please tell me what could be a bigger tragedy than this?

Krishna replied, Karna you are not the one who became a victim of the circumstances. Even I have also undergone grief and please understand;

1) Karna, I was born in a Jail.
2) Death was waiting for me even before my birth.
3) The night I was born, I was separated from my parents.
4) When all of you were being appreciated for your valor, I have not got even my basic education. I joined Gurukul of Rishi Sandipan only at the age of 16.
5) You are married to a girl of your choice. I didn't get the girl I loved.

6) I had to move my whole community from the banks of Yamuna to far off sea shore to save them from Jarasandh.

Even the incarnation of Vishnu had grief, disappointments and tragedies. Kiran, surrender yourself wholeheartedly to Krishna. Respect your parents, Abhimanyu parents and take care of yourself and the people around you.

ISKCON's advice was like, "A drowning man will clutch at a straw."

Preparations were being made for the cremation of Abhimanyu's dead body. Posters lined up the street of Civil lines home to martyred Abhimanyuv Singh. Shops remained closed in respect. Sweepers from Rohtak Municipal Corporation kept cleaning the litter every few hours in that locality where Abhimanyu lived most of his life.

The funeral procession from his house started at 9:30AM while the lane where Abhimanyu's family lived was cordoned off to traffic and heavy Police Bandobast and the Riot Police was stationed nearby. The family received condolence visits from Politicians, Bureaucrats and Celebrities, respected Citizens of the city. Thousands of people witnessed to pay respect to Abhimanyu in Coffin draped in Tricolour. Early in the morning the military truck decked with flowers and guarded by military men started from his house for last rites which was performed with full military honors later in the day.

Thousands of emotional onlookers lined up the roads on both sides and from building tops and terraces as they showered flowers on the Coffin, raising slogans of , "Major Abhimanyu Singh Amar Rahe! and Bharat Mata ki Jai!" waving the Indian Flags. Many women could be seen weeping. It was a proud moment for the family.

Though the parents of Abhimanyu and Kiran were crippled, they were in tears and were unable to console each other, they maintained the most difficult position of being parents of a gallant soldier. The funeral procession started at 10:00AM and reached Shiv dhaam crematorium at 12 noon. Abhimanyu's parents placed the wreaths on the body while holding back their tears and appealed to the people to maintain peace. Col. Ranjit Singh lit the funeral pyre at the crematorium and the last rites were performed.

Kiran was lost and she had a feeling that life has no meaning now. Kiran's mother Mrs.Rajbala Singh was taking care of her daughter.

# 28

It is crazy how fast time flies. It seems like yesterday when I was seeing Abhimanyu leaving the main gate of our house to resume his most loved duty at the J & K border. Kiran in her thoughts, "I haven't washed his regimental jacket and when I miss him a lot, I wear it. It still smells of him."

"I smile through my tears because I know what he would have wanted me to do. Like people say, if you haven't felt your soul being torn apart, you haven't really loved with all your heart". Though it hurts, I will always love him but at the same time, she was filled with anger and anguish.

"My heart still swells with pride every time my husband's name is mentioned but he laid his life for the nation, there has not been one day when I haven't contemplated suicide for the following situations."

1) Coping with persistent unpleasant memories.
2) Avoiding certain rooms or situations in the house.
3) Experiencing hallucinations where my dead husband was seen.
4) Still dealing with his personal effects like clothes and other belongings.

Kiran's outburst was an abuse to the people and for the reasons of war. She very vehemently and with a heavy heart said and wished, if wars could only happen, they should only happen to those ordering them and have to lead the battles in person with their families. She was evidently pointing out fingers on Politicians and Bureaucrats without actually naming them. Wars and invasions are very easy to begin and very difficult to end. Killing people and destroying countries have very long lived consequences and this would trigger intergenerational hatred and endless cycles of revenge. Again I am sorry to say that wars are usually commenced by those who face no consequences. Unfortunately there are 25000 war widows like me in India for no fault of theirs.

Kiran was fighting with herself but since there was no armour against fate, she was slowly coming to terms looking after her family and her own parents and doing her education obligation in Jawaharlal Nehru University for the welfare of the society.

# 29

There was a family function in Udayvir Singh's joint family which was attended by Kiran's parents, Kiran's in-laws and Abhinandan's parents in Meerut. It was close to one year after Abhimanyu's death but Kiran has not been in terms of normal life. Udayvir Singh was seeing his daughter in sick, tiring and quiet conditions. He was always getting the shock of his life beyond imagination, "My tiny little girl that has slept on my chest for days and years has come to this pathetic condition." He started crying loudly along with his wife Rajbala Singh. Memories of her childhood, her presence in parties, in and out of their home, her elementary school plays and her going to school in uniform, all started appearing in front of their eyes like a flashback of time. He thought what have I not done that I need to do for her? My daughter Kiran remained hung on every word I uttered.

Udayvir one day after the function left a note to Kiran as he couldn't speak his heart to her being a father that could create an embarrassment to both father and daughter.

My dear Kiran,

Your Papa is extremely painful for all the sufferings/ pain/trauma, my little darling daughter has gone through. There are certain things which can't be undone now but your Papa promises that he would only do right things and would ensure that my daughter will not have even a single drop of tears in her eyes. Mummy & Papa would like to settle their loving daughter and hence wants to marry you once again.

Kiran cried the whole night after reading her father's note. She didn't know how to react. After she stopped crying, she wrote,

Papa,

My love for Abhimanyu, a true love in being together in joys and pains holding each other in every sunshine and rain will give me enough strength to move on in life. I have responsibilities towards you, towards Abhimanyu parents to look after. I understand that Papa, moving from a relationship is one of the most difficult transitions in my life. One truth is almost universal, we will face this challenge at this point of time but at the same time. One thing is that I am not alone in this suffering. I will believe in myself and look at my life as a journey.

I would request you parents and parents in-laws to support me in all my endeavors in the days to come.

Udayvir Singh discussed Kiran's reply with Col. Ranjit Singh and they both agreed that the death of Abhimanyu is not just emotionally painful and traumatic but also brings about multiple trials and tribulations for Kiran. There is suddenly a vacuum in marital life and practical problems galore that need attention from the surviving wife.

Kiran is young at just 29 years and has natural body needs and just because she is a widow, it didn't mean that her life as a young wife had to dry. They both decided to remarry Kiran. Maybe a woman like Kiran was not born. She in spite of all the social problems remained calm, serene and tranquil though the families and society hardly consider the needs, opinions and desires of a woman whose husband has passed away but these two gentlemen never considered Kiran's remarriage as sacrilege.

Kiran reported that emotional turmoil started brewing soon after the death of Abhimanyu Singh on assurances of monetary compensation kept pouring in not only from the central government and army but also from the Haryana Govt. who promised a hefty sum as well as Govt. Job for Kiran, which she politely declined as she was already in a lucrative job at Jawaharlal Nehru University. Besides this a multinational corporation assured a big monetary compensation and the wife of a late actor-politician promised one acre of land to Kiran.

Kiran was hugely grateful to the Indian Army as they are not just limited to providing security to the country, it also plays an active role in the ideological discipling of the nation against any oppression to army wives.

The rural social situation in North India, complete with its strict social norms, joint family system, Patriarchal structure, low education levels and customs of levirate were all affected due to higher education of Kiran and it got a bigger Jolt following the payment of huge sum of money as compensation to the war widow. But the Patriarchal society looked for levirate marriage of Kiran.

Kiran's parents and her in-laws all wanted her to remarry and that's what Abhimanyu would have wanted her to be happy. They addressed Kiran, "We do not want to inflict pain on the loss of your husband." The reality was that they couldn't convince her. They again persuaded her saying that you have suffered a loss so terrible that we have no name for it but Kiran you have a long life to live and move on. This world is so cruel that they will not take a minute to name you a woman, frivolous, immoral and available.

I love my husband and the very thought of being physically close to anyone else puts me off and out. I have been in love with Abhimanyu since my early 20s and I just know that I would only want him even when I am widowed at 28.

Kiran knew her weakness and fears but probably no one understood her needs. She was feeling very scared and isolating in spite of a huge family of her parents and her in-laws. In Kiran's own words, "I am not sure, much needs to be said on this matter of my remarriage.

I am also a human, I most likely crave for some level of physical comfort and perhaps long for intimacy but I can't imagine the kind of closeness with anyone but my deceased husband.

She was bold in expressing herself.

Now Col. Ranjit Singh, father of stain Abhimanyu asked Kiran, why do you want to remain faithful to a GHOST? There is no rule like a woman is born only for one man. Your destiny is different and you have to live with your Karma.

KIRAN WAS STILL FIRM AND ADAMANT!

Her parents and Abhimanyu's parents were disappointed but not without a hope.

# 30

In this world specially in North India suffering of young widow women, the exploitation of women is quite prevalent. They are compelled to marry again. They are never given the opportunity to marry as per their choice but this Patriarchal society just dumps them to marry the younger brothers of their deceased husbands.

For Kiran, entering into a new relationship after she has been through the terrible pain of the demise of her husband just one year back could be both an intimidating and unexpectedly shocking new chapter in her life. Kiran now had a clear understanding of her boundaries and the level of independence.

She was in deep dilemma of marrying again

because;

1) She has not fallen in love with the prospective husband.
2) She has no financial dependency.
3) She wasn't feeling more than lust.

The only positive side was that both the families of her parents and in-laws were happy and she was too prepared to take care of them both financially and emotionally and she was not prepared to be called or considered inauspicious. Also both her parents and Abhimanyu's parents are now dreaming about Kiran to be married again to a perfect life partner and finding her happy even after.

In India, sacrificing everything to accept parents ' decision is a common phenomenon and Kiran was no exception to this and she unwillingly agreed to buy her parents' wish of marrying again though the thought of drawing Abhimanyu out of her heart and mind would take a lot of time. She respected………. THE UNFORGETTABLE TRUTH: "ALL RELATIONSHIPS END EVEN IN LONG TERM MARRIAGES, ONE OF THE TWO DIES BEFORE THE OTHER LEAVING THEIR PARTNER IN DEEP GRIEF."

Kiran at work was an over-achiever and aggressive power player. It was not for money. It was about a sense of self-importance, attention and validation but she accepted that she has no control over her parents decisions, actions and how they chose to treat her as a child.

She resigned to her fate and left everything to Udayvir Singh and Col. Ranjit Singh.

# 31

Under advice from another gynecologist Dr.Monika Mahajan considered it to be the last word in IVF treatment. Arya underwent all the detailed tests and analysis, she said in consultation with another two experts univocally that in order for a pregnancy to occur, the embryo must implant into the uterine lining (also known as Endometrium). Two hormones produced from the Ovaries thicken the uterine lining to develop the characteristics needed for implantation. Arya's uterine lining was very thin and not thickening in-spite of sufficient substitutes given. They further advised that a thin uterine lining is a risk for pregnancy and multiple miscarriages. The only sure option left is to use the services of a surrogate mother.

The final verdict of the panel of doctors confirming the infertility of Arya was a testing time for two relationships, husband and in-laws. The relationship between mother in-law and daughter in-law was crucial and was cascading towards climax during her extremely difficult journey of infertility and for Arya it was a time for lagging, taunting and judgmental attitude. Dr.Monika Mahajan advised Kirti Singh not to hurt Arya specially when she was vulnerable and already fighting another battle and requested her not to make Arya fight two battles of infertility and relationship at one time.

Under pressure from Kirti Singh and other relatives of the family, Virendra Singh, father of Abhinandan Singh imposed dictates without popular consent which were final and binding to the couple.

DICTATE NO.1 -Since Abhinandan is medically fit to father a child, he would be married again with a girl from a different family from the same caste.

DICTATE NO.2 -Arya would stay in the same house with full honour and dignity and she would be entitled to one-third of the property and valuables owned by Abhinandan

Singh. She would now be treated as a daughter of this family.

DICTATE NO.3 -Abhinandan and Arya would adopt the youngest son of Abhinandan's eldest sister legally and he would be the heir apparent of Abhinandan and would inherit all the rights and privileges of his son.

DICTATE NO.4 -No other woman would be used to get a Vaarish through traditional or Gestational surrogacy. This is against our traditions and religious customs.

Manipulations started in the members of family and relatives out of greed. But Abhinandan was sternly against his second marriage as he was already married so there is no question of his marrying again. Arya will stay in this house as my wife and she would be a legal and dignified daughter in-law for you both.

# 32

Mrs. Veermati Singh knew that her son would not come. The loss is irreplaceable. She could not stand the miseries of her daughter in-law who is just 29 years. She has the right to be happy in life so she decided to get Kiran married. She again explained to Kiran that life does not stop for anyone and encouraged her daughter in-law to start a new life and started exploring the suitable match for Kiran.

Veermati had a son Aditya Singh just two years younger to Abhimanyu and six months older than Kiran. Aditya was well, different from others. He was handsome. He had that appearance which could make him stand out in the crowd. He was fair. His eyes were deep and expressive. His smile which reached up to his eyes flaunted his modesty and humility. He was handsome from the depth of his eyes to the gentle expression of his voice. He was a shade closer to his elder brother Abhimanyu. Professionally he was the team leader in a renowned software multi-national company based in Gurugram.

Both Veermati Singh, Col. Ranjit Singh met Udayvir Singh and Rajbala Singh and proposed a marriage of Kiran with Aditya Singh, younger brother of Maj. Abhimanyu Singh. In North India specially Haryana and Western UP for a very long time if a man died without a child, it was common for the man's younger unmarried brother to marry the widow in order to provide an heir for the deceased. Accordingly, a widow would marry a brother-in-law and the first son produced in that union was considered the legal descendant of her dead husband.

There were several reasons for the prevalence of this tradition. Firstly it was a way of ensuring the well-being of the widow and to provide security of sorts. Secondly this kind of union also took place to provide an heir for the deceased and to continue the lineage of the family. Thirdly and most importantly, this was done so that land or property owned by the deceased husband would continue to stay in his family.

Kiran's parents didn't have any reservations keeping

in mind the psychological and sociological impact of this levirate marriage but they left this to be decided by Kiran herself.

Kiran had all reservations to marry her brother in-law for two strong reasons;

1) She has treated Aditya like her brother all along and he too used to say that the wife of elder brother is like a mother to him.
2) Such marriages called levirate cannot respect the Institution of Marriage in case the child born in that union is a girl child.
3) Kiran feels that the intention of marriage may deeply be influenced by the web of greed for money and properties.

Hearing this Veermati Singh appeared to be irritated as she had a feeling of disobedience from Kiran. Kiran only expressed her own apprehension and never said that she would not marry Aditya. Aditya himself was utterly confused as he believed that whatever Kiran has said about her relationship with him, is absolutely right and was respected till today. Veermati admonished Aditya and asked him that he may be right as said in our religious epics but did he actually treat her like his biological mother? Aditya had no answer.

Kiran excused herself from this discussion with an

excuse of needing time to revert.

She shut herself in a closed room and after giving the situation a serious thought, she wanted to make an analysis of the happenings;

1) Whether her mother-in-law is genuinely thinking of Kiran's welfare?
2) Aditya is good looking and professionally very well settled so why was he made to agree for an alliance with Kiran? He can get a much better match.
3) Kiran's father in-law looks genuine, takes care of Kiran.
4) Whether her mother-in-law has developed some sort of greed for Kiran's finances and properties?

Kiran was considerably rich now due to the huge compensation from various agencies like Indian Army, Central and State Governments and many national and international multi-corporates including one acre of land all valued at approx. 10 Crores of Indian Rupees.

It's human tendency that everyone is tempted at some point in their life but in people with a strong fear of deprivation, greed can become a dominant pattern. Greed is about never being satisfied with whatever her mother in-law has, always wanting and expecting more. It is an insatiable hunger.

Ever since Abhimanyu died, there were some

evident changes (especially after huge compensation started flowing) in her behavior and lifestyle. She started feeling a bit insecure. She started having a strong possessive attitude towards Aditya and her husband and obviously not for Kiran. There seemed a strong possibility of her spying on Kiran, specifically keeping a sharp eye on Kiran spending some money which was never there when Abhi was there. To the outside world, she used to act all loving and would shower her with love, she would always praise Kiran and show what a lovely relationship both of them shared.

It was evident that the seeds of deep rooted suspicion between both of them were sown. She developed the first dislike for levirate marriage with Aditya.

She still had nothing adverse against any of the members of the family.

The biggest apprehension Veermati had was about Kiran marrying anyone other than Aditya would deprive her family with the money and property which Kiran owns now including the pension of the slain Major Abhimanyu Singh. She never wanted Kiran to marry anyone else other than Aditya. According to her the entire compensation goes out of this family to another family where she would be married. This was as per the Army Act 1950.

## 33

Kiran's sense of duty and gratitude towards her Uncle Ajay Singh's family was ingrained deep within her. She knew that they had played a vital role in shaping her into the responsible citizen she was today, and she felt obligated to reciprocate their kindness by providing support and respect whenever necessary. Kiran's love for her own family, including her parents, in-laws, and Arya's parents, was equally strong. She valued their opinions and always strived to improve her relationship with them. Kiran understood that emotional intelligence was crucial in maintaining strong bonds, and she made it a point to work on it.

However, when Arya received Dictate No.1 from Virendra Singh, she was thrown into a state of shock and grief. The news was too much for her to bear, and she began to exhibit abnormal behavior. She was consumed by despair, loneliness, and a sense of detachment. Kiran was heartbroken to see her beloved sister in such a state and was determined to bring her back to her old self. She knew it would be a daunting task, but Kiran was up for the challenge. She was willing to do whatever it takes, right or wrong, to bring Arya out of the well of despair. Kiran explored every possible option and was persistent and patient in her efforts to help her sister.

Kiran had an extreme urge to hug her sister Arya. Arya felt that Kiran cares about her a lot as a sister as Arya was hurt by everyone at home except Abhimnandan but Kiran proved to be her savior and as a result Arya felt a bit warm and secure. She noticed that Arya is upset, needing Kiran for comfort and to be supportive and helpful. Kiran offered her a shoulder to cry on and in fact she herself started crying loudly.

Kiran took Arya to Ambience Mall, the biggest in Gurugram and tried many things to make her laugh including inside jokes which could only be discussed between two sisters of the same age and are prohibited in Public or with other people. Kiran even tried to impersonate Virendra Singh passing those judgmental dictates. Fresh air away from their homes and company with her sister Kiran made Arya a bit at ease. In the process, Kiran discussed all the dictates passed on by Virendra Singh and rejected them out right without giving any importance. She would find the solution with Abhinandan Singh after discussing everything in person including adoption and surrogacy.

Arya at least visibly looked assured and cheerful.

# 34

Abhinandan Singh was very fond of Kiran Singh so he willingly agreed to meet her in a luxury restaurant in South Extension, Delhi for lunch. As scheduled Abhinandan reached the restaurant at 1 PM and Kiran was waiting for him with a bouquet of nice different Orchid flowers. It was a mere coincidence and pleasant surprise that Abhinandan Singh also brought a bouquet of Orchid flowers. They sat in a cozy corner of the restaurant. Kiran took the initiative of starting a conversation.

Kiran picked up her phone and dialed Abhinandan's number. "Hello, Abhinandan, how are you?" She greeted him.

"I'm doing alright, Kiran," Abhinandan replied.

"How about you?"

"I can't complain. But listen, I can't call you Abhi because I had my own Abhi, Major Abhimanyu Singh," Kiran explained.

Abhinandan understood. "I was scared to hear about him, but he has left a wonderful legacy and pleasant memories to strengthen you to move on," he said.

"Yes, I am living on and surviving on his memories and the truth of his gallant and brave nature. It was a source of immense pride when I was told that it was because of his solo efforts and courage that we were able to defend the sovereignty of our country," Kiran said.

Abhinandan nodded in agreement. "Yes, Arya and I were very sad on his departure, but our chests swelled with pride. I met him once or twice, but I must admit that he won over my heart as he treated me as his thick friend rather than a brother-in-law."

"How is Arya?" Kiran asked with concern.

"You know better, Kiran. She partially smiles only after hearing your name. She is passing through a difficult phase of her life. I take special care of her, but somebody or the other in the family gives her a reason to grieve. I console her a lot, but ultimately she is a human being," Abhinandan replied.

Kiran listened attentively. "What have you thought

about her problems and ways to keep her happy and insulated from the toxic people around her?" she asked.

"I have decided to move out of that house and the ambiance," Abhinandan said.

"But that's not a solution, Abhinandan. It would be at the cost of making your parents unhappy," Kiran pointed out.

"I explored other options, but you know that my parents are dead against it," Abhinandan replied.

"It is a complex situation, Abhinandan. Please tell me very frankly, what have you decided about your second marriage or surrogacy?" Kiran asked, her voice gentle but direct.

"Kiran, I love my wife Arya more than life itself. She is the center of my universe and the love of my life, so most of the options suggested by my father are not acceptable to me. Frankly speaking, I can't leave Arya in a lurch where she would feel absolutely helpless. As far as surrogacy is concerned, the gestational surrogacy is medically ruled out, and you need another woman as a surrogate for traditional surrogacy, which my parents would not accept," Abhinandan said.

Kiran understood the weight of Abhinandan's decision. "Would you be able to stand against your parents if they impose any or all the dictates?" she asked.

"I have clearly and sternly conveyed my firm decision that I will never respect all of their decisions," Abhinandan replied.

Kiran thought for a moment before bringing up another topic. "Are you aware of Levirate and Sororate marriages followed in Haryana, Western U.P., and Rajasthan? I am also being tried and persuaded for my Levirate marriage with the younger brother of Abhimanyu," she said.

"Yes, I am aware of these two types of marriage. Some are legal, and some are semi-legal. What's your opinion in this regard?" Abhinandan asked.

"I have not given it serious thought. Personally, I have my own reservations, but how long could I resist the wishes of Abhimanyu's parents, my parents, and Arya's parents? Arya said.

Abhinandan nodded slowly, his expression thoughtful. "I understand. It's a difficult situation for both of us. We have to make sure that Arya is happy and taken care of, but we also have to respect our parents' wishes."

Kiran sighed. "I know. It's not easy. But we have to find a way."

Abhinandan smiled faintly. "I have faith in us. We'll figure it out."

Kiran smiled back, feeling a glimmer of hope. "Yes,

we will. We're family, after all."

They continued to talk, brainstorming ideas and discussing their options. Though the road ahead was uncertain and full of challenges, they both knew that they could count on each other to navigate it together. They had a healthy discussion and a very sumptuous vegetarian lunch and left.

After coming back home Kiran took her mother and Arya's mother in confidence and revealed everything in details regarding her lunch in discussions with Abhinandan Singh.

# 35

One fine morning, Aditya's parents had gone to Chandigarh for a family function and some official assignment. Kiran and Aditya were on the dining table for breakfast before leaving for their offices.

Kiran sat across from Aditya, feeling a twinge of guilt at the conversation they were having. She knew that her in-laws were discussing a Levirate marriage for her with Aditya, after her husband Abhimanyu's tragic death. But she also understood Aditya's predicament and couldn't help but sympathize with him.

"Adi, are you aware that Mummy, Daddy are talking about your marriage to me?" Kiran finally spoke up, breaking the silence.

Aditya nodded, a resigned expression on his face.

"Yes, Kiran, I should call you Bhabhi (Sister in-law) now. I am aware of everything going around in our house for a Levirate marriage. But are you aware that I am seeing Ruchi Singh, my colleague, for a long-term relationship with her?"

Kiran's eyebrows shot up in surprise. "No, I had no idea. You dropped hints?"

Aditya nodded again. "I dropped sufficient hints, I don't know whether you picked up even one? My parents are absolutely ignorant of this, and for me to convince them or even reveal it to them looks like building objects immune to gravity."

Kiran couldn't help but chuckle at the analogy. "I'll try to talk to them, but I can't make any promises. They see me as your future wife, after all."

Aditya's eyes sparkled with gratitude. "Thank you. You are like my Mom, being the wife of my elder brother Abhimanyu. HA HA HA."

As Kiran delved into the daunting task of initiating a conversation with her in-laws on Aditya's side, a wave of devastation washed over him. He found himself caught in a precarious position, having already discovered his perfect partner in a fellow software colleague. Aditya braced himself for his parents' anticipated disapproval, especially considering the prevailing circumstances and their strong inclination towards arranging his Levirate marriage with Kiran. Being deeply attached to his parents and holding a genuine affection for his sister-in-law, Kiran, he yearned for their blessing to marry Ruchi Singh, all while remaining loyal to the person he had chosen to share the rest of his life with. This internal conflict tore at his heart, leaving him utterly torn with a capital T.

Aditya's predicament was as intricate as it was emotionally charged. On one hand, he cherished his familial bond and desired his parents' acceptance and support in his pursuit of a life with Ruchi. On the other hand, he wrestled with his loyalty to Kiran, understanding the significance of their shared history and the weighty expectations that had been placed upon them. The conflicting desires to honor his own happiness and remain true to his commitments left Aditya in a state of profound turmoil.

As he navigated these treacherous emotional waters, Aditya yearned for a resolution that would appease his own heart, honor his loved ones, and forge a harmonious path forward. The struggle to reconcile his personal desires with the expectations and traditions ingrained within his family created a profound internal dilemma, one that demanded careful consideration and a delicate balancing act. In this intense period of introspection, Aditya grappled with the weight of his choices, acutely aware of the immense impact they would have on both his own life and the intricate web of relationships that surrounded him.

The relentless tug-of-war between love, loyalty, and familial obligations persisted within Aditya's soul, intensifying his emotional turmoil. With each passing moment, he found himself yearning for a resolution that would align his heart's desires with the expectations of his family, fostering a sense of unity and understanding. The depth of his devotion to both his partner, Ruchi, and his family fueled his determination to find a way to bridge the divide and bring harmony to the complex dynamics at play.

As the hours turned into days and the days into weeks, Aditya traversed the labyrinthine corridors of his emotions, seeking solace and guidance. He remained resolute in his pursuit of a solution that would honor his own happiness while also respecting the bonds that tied him to his loved ones. This delicate dance between personal fulfillment and familial unity propelled him forward, undeterred by the challenges that lay ahead.

In the crucible of conflicting emotions, Aditya's unwavering resolve to navigate this intricate situation with sensitivity and compassion marked him as a true seeker of harmony. The weight of his torn heart only fueled his determination to discover a path that would uphold both his personal aspirations and his profound reverence for family values. With steadfast courage, he embarked on a journey of self-reflection and open communication, with the hope of ultimately finding a resolution that would reconcile his love for Ruchi with the deep familial bonds he cherished.

Aditya instead of talking directly to his parents talked to Kiran to help understand him and make parents understand too. Kiran very calmly and respectfully put forward her views about this alliance to Col. Ranjit Singh and Kirti Singh and tried to know their objection. Their first reaction was a big NO for obvious reasons but on persistent requests, they both agreed to really get to know Ruchi. Kiran was able to convince them to forget the opposition which was based on misunderstanding and misconceptions. Aditya was happy to meet his parents with a smiling face subsequently and helped his parents and Kiran to become more comfortable with Aditya's partner. Ruchi's parents invited them out to dinner and then some sporting event in a 5 Star Deluxe Hotel.

In the dining hall of the hotel, things were pretty cool. They seemed to be happy after seeing Ruchi and her parents. They were particularly happy seeing their background, most importantly their caste same as Col. Ranjit Singh's. Col. seemed agreeable but told them, the things will proceed after we settle our daughter in-law Kiran, Abhimanyu's wife.

# 36

Both Rajbala Singh and Veena Singh discussed the future of their daughters Kiran and Arya along with their husbands Udayvir Singh and Virendra Singh. They left Abhinandan's parents away for the initial discussion because they feared that Virendra Singh would insist on imposition of those four dictates. They had a deep conversation about feelings, anxieties, fears, failures and hopes for their daughters Kiran and Arya. In front of them were two serious problems of settling Kiran and finding the most appropriate solution to Arya's most difficult problem of not having a kid for continuity of her family lineage.

Veena Singh suddenly mentioned about one marriage in her native village that such marriage has taken place in which a woman was not able to produce kids and her husband was married to her own sister who was unmarried and both the sisters are living together amicably with no sibling rivalry and the first woman loves her sister's son as her own biological son.

Initially a lot of tongues were wagging and also there were few jealous people who were always talking that this arrangement is illegal and the couple will be penalized by the Court of law. According to them, a man can't marry his second wife if the first wife is alive. Some were naming it as immoral, some were saying that it is an emotional atrocity on the first wife. Later it was clarified to these illiterate beings that this marriage called Sororate Marriage is valid as per Indian Constitution and Indian Penal Code that says, the intended person can marry the sister of his first wife in event of her death or in event of the first wife being infertile. It was then universally accepted.

The fingers of Rajbala Singh tightened convulsively with a jolt, Veena Singh gave. It was like a bomb shell falling on Rajbala Singh, Udayvir Singh and Ajay Singh. They were all compelled to give it a serious thought. They all univocally said, we can't even think about it without taking our both daughters in confidence and seeking their consent. Then they decided to talk to them individually.

| | |
|---|---|
| Rajbala | -Arya, who do you trust the most? |
| Arya | -Of course Kiran, she fills all the emptiness in my heart. I am so thankful to have her in my life. |
| Veena Singh | -Kiran, how big of a support are you and will be in future to Arya? |

Kiran said, "She is a special gift from the heavens to me. Her smile now warms my heart and her presence makes me whole. I love her more than my life after Abhimanyu Singh."

Kiran further added,"I understand, the topic is awkward but I have no alternative but to talk to you. Sometimes, I feel that we would cross a huge social boundary. This is the practice of Sororate Marriage when a man marries the sister of his wife in case, either she is dead or she is infertile contrary to Levirate Marriage, where a widow marries her late husband's brother as the case of Aditya being proposed for me."

As the echoes of the forthcoming arrangement reached their ears, a wave of emotion washed over the hearts of both Kiran and Arya, two sisters bound by an unbreakable bond. In that tender moment, Kiran's gaze met Arya's, and she expressed a sentiment that had long lingered within her soul. She acknowledged her sensitivity towards the notion that life often unfolds without the presence of clear-cut "firsts" or solitary triumphs.

In a world brimming with countless stories and infinite paths, Kiran recognized the inherent interconnectedness that weaves through the fabric of existence. She understood that the tapestry of life, with all its intricate threads, seldom adheres to rigid hierarchies of precedence or exclusivity. Each person's journey is unique, yet deeply intertwined with the journeys of others, creating a symphony of shared experiences and interwoven destinies.

With heartfelt sincerity, Kiran conveyed to Arya the essence of her realization, painting a portrait of empathy and understanding. She recognized that in the grand tapestry of life, triumphs are rarely solitary and achievements are rarely isolated. Rather, they emerge as collective efforts, harmoniously shaped by the influence and presence of others.

In her introspection, Kiran sought to honor the countless souls who have walked similar paths, acknowledging their contributions and celebrating the beauty of shared experiences. By embracing the interconnectedness of human existence, she invited a broader perspective that transcended notions of exclusivity and celebrated the interdependence that binds us all.

As the emotional weight of the impending event hung in the air, Kiran's words served as a gentle reminder that within the tapestry of life, the boundaries of "firsts" and "onlys" blur, revealing a richer tapestry woven with the threads of countless lives. And in this recognition, Kiran and Arya found solace, strengthened by the realization that their journey, intertwined with others, holds a beauty that transcends the confines of singular achievements.

# 37

Kiran was acutely aware of the prevailing tension within their intertwined families, a tension stemming from various underlying reasons: her own Levirate marriage, Arya's struggle with infertility, and the countless intricacies that often accompany such delicate situations. She possessed a deep understanding that these complex problems couldn't be resolved through explosive outbursts or raised voices. Instead, a deliberate and conscientious approach was necessary, one that required every family member to actively participate in finding common ground.

Conflicts, as Kiran realized, often arise when individuals fail to grasp or perhaps intentionally overlook the nuanced expectations and intricacies of the problems at hand. Even within the closest-knit families, disagreements and divergent viewpoints are inevitable, further fueling the flames of potential discord. This reality was not lost on the four immediate families—Abhimanyu's, Kiran's, Arya's, and Abhinandan—who, in their own unique ways, found themselves regularly exposed to simmering family conflicts.

For Kiran, navigating these tense conversations hinged on her approach—an approach characterized by fearlessness and an unwavering commitment to honesty. She resolved to engage in open dialogue with each member of the family, recognizing the transformative power of genuine conversation. With a mindful intention to mend fractured relationships and forge a path toward understanding, Kiran embarked on her journey, commencing her heartfelt conversations with her in-laws.

In these intimate exchanges, she sought to create an atmosphere of compassion, empathy, and vulnerability. Kiran understood that true resolution could only be attained through active listening, sincere expressions of thoughts and emotions, and a genuine willingness to bridge the gaps that had emerged. Through these earnest conversations, she aimed to foster an environment where differing perspectives could be heard and respected, paving the way for harmonious resolutions.

Kiran's commitment to addressing the underlying tensions within their extended family network reflected her profound understanding of the importance of open and honest communication. By initiating these transformative dialogues, she endeavored to rebuild frayed bonds, nurture understanding, and pave the way for a future marked by unity and harmony. In taking these courageous steps, Kiran demonstrated her unwavering dedication to fostering familial peace and fostering a supportive environment for all.

Kiran sat across from her father, Col. Ranjit Singh, in the quiet of their living room. Her heart raced as she prepared to broach a delicate topic with her father. "Dad, what if I don't agree with you for a Levirate marriage with Aditya? Actually, I have already conveyed my disagreement with you."

Col. Ranjit Singh listened intently to his daughter's words before responding. "Kiran, I agree with you for not marrying Aditya for Ruchi and your treatment of Aditya, but there are still certain things you will need to consider. The Armed Force Tribunal (AFT) has declared regulations that deprive a soldier's widow of a Liberalized Family Pension (LFP) if she remarries anyone other than her husband's brother as void. Secondly, we don't need you to be away from us. You will remain our daughter instead of your daughter in-law."

Kiran took a deep breath and responded, "Dad, first of all, I have not decided to remarry anyone at this stage. In the event of my marriage to any other person, I'll leave my entire property, compensation from various agencies, and divide into two portions, 50% of which would be given to you and 50% to my parents. The one acre land, I will give it to you only. As regards to LFP, the regulation of Armed Forces Tribunal 1950 has been amended and according to the latest amendment in a major relief to widows of martyrs. The defense ministry has decided to do away with a condition that they have to marry the deceased husband's brother. The ministry has now decided that the widow can now marry anyone and will still get all the dues including Pension. Whether I marry or I don't, you would always remain my in-law and it would be my responsibility to look after you."

Col. Ranjit Singh nodded in understanding. "You would always remain more than our daughter and your kids would remain our grandchildren."

"Papa, I will remain your little girl till my last breath. I will look after you both like kids. I would never give you an opportunity when I could refuse any of your words, instructions wrong or right," Kiran said with determination.

Udayvir Singh, Kiran's uncle, spoke up. "I know beta. You are an armor for our existence."

Kiran turned to Virendra Singh, her other uncle. "Virendra Uncle, may I request you to be kind to Arya and not press for any unreasonable dictates. I fully endorse your views of having a grandson for the continuity of your lineage, but you still have Deepak Singh, your second son, and God willing, he would provide you your family heir. It is just unfortunate that Arya would not be the one to do so. It is none of her fault as God only has made her like that. You can also think of a second marriage of Abhinandan Singh if he agrees which would be legal as per the law of the land, could be a bit immoral for him."

Virendra Singh listened to Kiran's words and responded, "Kiran, we respect you for your concern and assure you that no injustice would be done to Arya either in our treatment of her or for any financial constraints."

Kiran expressed her gratitude, "I would be grateful to you forever uncle."

Turning to her other uncle, Ajay Singh, Kiran said, "My dear Ajay Uncle, you need not take any stress for Arya as she has got a sister who is her reflection in me. I would share all her sorrows and joys."

"We are so confident about you, but still God has not been kind to Arya.I wish she would share her pains with you all the time and she would have your shoulders to cry."

Kiran nodded, "She will never need my shoulders to cry.

Kiran gazed at her younger sister, her eyes filled with love and determination. "She will never need my shoulders to cry," Kiran said firmly. "On the other hand, I will ensure that this situation never comes."

Arya looked up at her sister, her eyes shining with emotion. "Kiran, I am sure you have confidence in me that I would be more than present in your life and of course leaving some space for Abhinandan."

"Of course, I do," Kiran said reassuringly. "You fill all the vacuum in my life and would continue doing that, but is it possible for you to remain with me all the 24 hours? It will make me 100 percent stress and trouble-free."

Kiran paused, considering her sister's request. "24 hours? Yes, if it is humanly possible," she said finally, her voice full of conviction. "I will always be here for you, Arya. Always."

Udayvir Singh, Ajay Singh and Virendra Singh were prompted to deep thoughts and also in a thought provoking situation. They all started looking at each other. Hope it was like, "Coming events cast their shadows before." They even consulted Col. Ranjit Singh for Kiran's marriage to Abhinandan Singh but who would bell the cat, was a question yet to be answered.

# 38

In the intricate tapestry of Hindu culture, the institution of marriage reigns as a sacred and revered union, bearing profound significance within the fabric of society. Embedded within its essence lies the understanding that this alliance extends far beyond the realm of individual bonds, encompassing the harmonious convergence of two families. A patriarchal foundation has laid the groundwork for this sacred union, permeating our societal framework since time immemorial, manifesting itself in various forms throughout history.

However, for Kiran, the rigid constraints that once confined widows to a life of seclusion and solitude have engendered adverse consequences, creating a fertile ground for immorality to flourish. The restriction on widow remarriage, once deemed an ingrained societal norm, has cast a shadow over the lives of these women, exposing them to the perils of sexual exploitation and pushing them towards the fringes of society. The unfortunate consequence has been a surge in the proliferation of prostitution, a deplorable outcome that has contributed to the erosion of women's general status within Hindu society.

Yet, amidst the bleak landscape, glimmers of hope emerge as tireless efforts spearheaded by social reformists and enlightened individuals strive to dismantle the barriers that shackle widows to a life of isolation. Over time, the tides of change have gradually swept across the cultural landscape, carrying with them an evolved perspective. Widowed individuals are no longer shackled by societal condemnation; rather, their remarriage is increasingly embraced as a rightful choice, devoid of moral wrongdoing.

This seismic shift in perception stands testament to the resilience of a society propelled by the relentless pursuit of progress and equality. The concerted endeavors of those who champion social reform and the growing influence of education have laid a foundation upon which widows can rebuild their lives, unburdened by the weight of societal stigma. The very notion of widow remarriage, once seen as taboo, has been reimagined, infused with a newfound sense of acceptance and understanding.

As these winds of change continue to gust, a glimmer of optimism permeates the Hindu society, heralding a future where the shackles of widowhood are replaced by the promise of a second chance at love and companionship. Through compassionate discourse and collective enlightenment, the status quo has been challenged, ushering in a transformative era that fosters empowerment, inclusivity, and the restoration of dignity for widows.

In the grand tapestry of cultural evolution, widow remarriage represents a paradigm shift, an embodiment of society's relentless pursuit of justice and the emancipation of women. It serves as a beacon of hope, illuminating a path towards a future where love knows no bounds, and the indomitable spirit of humanity triumphs over archaic traditions.

They did consider Kiran's marriage with Abhinandan Singh but nobody talked to him for his acceptance. Rajbala Singh and Veena Singh called Abhinandan and asked him point blank whether he would accept Kiran as his religiously accepted wife? He very thoughtfully replied "I have always respected Kiran and I am a huge fan of hers. Now moving from respect to love would be a long journey for me. I am sure I'll complete the journey with Arya, come what may.

Before Udayvir Singh expresses his wish as a dictate to Kiran, he wanted Kiran, Arya and Abhinandan to discuss among themselves and clarify all their aspirations. They asked them to go in a separate room and decide the alliance by themselves only. Kiran told Arya that "I am marrying Abhinandan Singh with your consent for following reasons;

1) It will protect the prestige and status of the family.
2) It will keep you and me happy.
3) It will foster the sense of unity in the family.
4) It will keep all the property in the family.
5) We will have no hatred and jealousy for each other.
6) My first child with Abhinandan will be your's and it will continue the lineage of the Abhinandan family.
7) You will have no choice of difference to other children of Abhinandan at all.
8) We would share everything equally, be it properly, husband and any other luxury.
9) I will be your caretaker and you will be my caretaker.
10) Abhinandan will never be partial to you or to me too.
11) Abhinandan will be considered the main breadwinner and we are his subordinates.

12) Our relationship among you, me and Abhinandan Singh will be permanent. Its aim would not merely be physical pleasure but spiritual advancement.
13) In the event of the death of any one of us, there would not be any remarriage. For us duties automatically would come from the circumstances and mutual understanding. Nobody could forcibly dictate us of our duties, we will be free to think based on our wants and needs.

Kiran -Arya, do you have anything else to add or subtract?

Arya -We have shared everything in our lives and I feel that both of us can share our husband also . The three of us would remain close friends and I can't think of existing without one another.

Kiran -Arya, what about the Hindu Marriage Act which states that a man cannot marry for the second time, without divorcing the first wife.

Arya -The Act also says that a man may marry for the second time if his first wife is not in position to give him a child. Even if it is not true, "Love is above everything, we three have followed our hearts."

Abhinandan has already expressed his happiness

for this triangular alliance.

Udayvir Singh then asked Kiran to marry Abhinandan Singh which was the last word. They finally married and Arya did the rest. Remember a wife is a woman who joined the journey of her life to make it beautiful and successful. Kiran was not sharing the husband for the sake of lust but with a very positive goal.

It became a most loving family. The most precious thing for all three of them was their SELF RESPECT.

# 39

They became a beautiful family with the support and encouragement to all the members and for everyone the family became a never ending source of love, happiness and deep understanding. Each one of them was sure that these family members would stand at their side even during the most challenging trials and tribulations. Arya's health and mental status improved like anything which was a welcome change for the family. Abhinandan was performing the role of head of the family having all meals together. Nobody could prove a better coordinator than Kiran herself. She ensured that the bond that links their true family was not one of blood but of respect and joy in each other's life and the reason for this bond was love and self respect of everybody. In a way it was true "You don't choose your family, they are God's gift to you as you are to them." The love between them was patient, kind. It didn't have a place for envy, boast and pride and always rejoiced with the truth. It was all about the quality and finding a happy balance between work, friends and family. Kiran was anchoring the entire operation of the family. Everyone was thanking her without expressing it in words and body language.

They celebrated all the festivals and events of the family and society. The latest being the celebration of KARWA CHAUTH. It was a one day festival. Both Arya and Kiran observed a fast from sunrise to moonrise and prayed for the well-being and longevity of their husbands. They both sang songs related to KARWA CHAUTH and just waited. There was an anxious wait for the moonrise. As soon as the moon was sighted, they offered prayers to the moon. They both followed all the rituals until moonrise. They looked at the moon through a sieve and offered water and Mathari to the moon and from the same sieve they together saw Abhinandan and prayed for his well-being. Abhinandan took water, sweets and Matharies and fed both of his wives. Interestingly Abhinandan also observed fast from sunrise to moonrise with his wives.

# 40

As Kiran's journey through motherhood unfolded, she found herself immersed in a tapestry of hopeful anticipation. In the realm of age-old wisdom, certain signs and omens whispered secrets of imminent good fortune, casting a flickering light upon her path. Tradition taught that only a chosen few were bestowed with the gift of luck and prosperity, while the rest relied solely on the fruits of their tireless labor to forge their own happiness.

Yet, within the depths of Kiran's being, a delicate balance emerged, intertwining the threads of both fortune and diligent effort. While she ardently embraced the belief in the power of hard work, she couldn't deny the inexplicable occurrences that seemed to herald a deeper force at play. In those fleeting moments when the universe seemed to whisper its secrets, Kiran found solace in the notion that luck, in its ethereal form, danced alongside her unwavering dedication.

Acknowledging the intricate dance between chance and effort, Kiran recognized that certain phenomena, if noticed at the right juncture, could serve as auspicious omens, heralding the arrival of positivity and abundance. It was as if the universe bestowed subtle markers, inviting her to take notice and embrace the forthcoming blessings. Such signs, though ethereal in nature, sparked within her a renewed belief in the existence of luck and fortune.

In the tapestry of life's myriad experiences, Kiran's steadfast faith in both luck and the power of her own actions intermingled harmoniously. With each passing day, she traversed the delicate tightrope, navigating the realms of destiny and determination. While she remained an ardent believer in the boundless potential of hard work, the synchronicities and serendipities that punctuated her journey lent credence to the notion that unseen forces of luck and fortune did indeed cast their shimmering influence upon her life.

In this delicate balance between cosmic forces and human agency, Kiran found herself as a witness to the extraordinary interplay of destiny and personal effort.

Her unwavering belief in the existence of luck and fortune grew stronger with each passing day, bolstered by the signs and whispers that danced around her. She embraced the understanding that life's tapestry is woven with both visible and invisible threads, and that the convergence of these forces holds the promise of a future brimming with boundless possibilities.

As Kiran embarked upon the journey of motherhood, she carried within her heart the harmonious fusion of luck and hard work, a testament to her unwavering faith in the intricate symphony of the universe. And in the gentle whispers of serendipity, she found solace, knowing that the interplay of cosmic forces and her own efforts would guide her towards a destiny adorned with abundant blessings.

1) She saw a coconut the moment she woke up in the morning.
2) She also saw a white cow grazing in her compound.
3) She saw a lot of greenery in fields, in the garden.
4) She also saw a milkman with milk and curd.
5) She heard the sound of Shankh (Conch) and temple bells after she woke up.
6) For the first time, she saw a sugarcane juice vendor with a lot of sugarcanes.

Embraced by the unwavering faith she held in the

divine, Kiran found solace in the assurance that a bright and abundant destiny awaited her. As a testament to this celestial reassurance, she was blessed with the arrival of a beautiful baby boy, an embodiment of hope and promise. In the wake of this joyous occasion, Arya, ever the devoted caretaker, showered both Kiran and the newborn with unwavering love and tender care.

Immersed in the rich tapestry of Hindu customs and traditions, Kiran and Arya embarked upon the sacred journey of NAMKARAN SANSKAR, a ceremonial rite conducted on the twelfth day after the birth of the child. Adorned with the intricate rituals and timeless customs, this auspicious occasion resonated with profound significance. With utmost reverence, Kiran entrusted the precious gift of her baby boy into Arya's loving embrace, recognizing her as the true mother, the harbinger of a new generation destined to carry forth the noble lineage and legacy of their family.

On a serendipitous twist of fate, this joyous event unfolded on Arya's own birthday, creating an enchanting convergence of celebrations. As Kiran bestowed upon Arya a present beyond measure, she gifted her not only the undeniable love and attention of a devoted sister but also the precious gift of motherhood itself. In the timeless bonds of family, the elders of Kiran's, Arya's, Abhinandan, and Abhimanyu's lineage bestowed their blessings upon the young boy, enveloping him in the warmth of ancestral wisdom and collective love.

It was on this auspicious occasion that the newborn was lovingly christened Anmol, an appellation befitting his immense worth and the cherished place he held within their hearts. As the journey of life unfolded, he would come to be known as Aryakiran Singh, a name that intertwined the legacies of both Kiran and Arya, symbolizing the harmonious merging of their destinies.

In the embrace of motherhood, Arya blossomed, a radiant and proud figure, empowered by the profound love and responsibility bestowed upon her. With every tender touch and nurturing act, she embodied the essence of motherhood, a testament to her unwavering devotion and the unbreakable bond that linked her to the precious soul she held in her arms. Together, Kiran and Arya embarked upon a journey marked by love, strength, and the boundless possibilities that lay ahead for their growing family.

# *Characters*

| | |
|---|---|
| Kiran Singh | Kiran Singh |
| Udayvir Singh | Kiran's Father |
| Rajbala Singh | Kiran's Mother |
| Rajshree | Kiran's Maternal Aunt |
| Joe Fernandes | Kiran's Class Teacher |
| Aryaman | Kiran's Cousin Brother |
| Arya | Kiran's Cousin Sister |
| Abhimanyu Singh | Kiran's Husband |
| Abhinandan Singh | Arya's Husband |
| Col. Ranjit Singh | Abhimanyu's Father |
| Mrs.Veermati Singh | Abhimanyu's Mother |
| Aditya Singh | Abhimanyu's Brother |
| Virendra Singh | Abhinandan's Father |
| Kirti Singh | Abhinandan's Mother |
| Deepak Singh | Abhinandan's Brother |
| Lt. Col. Krishnamurthy | Comm. Officer, Pumpore |
| Ajay Singh | Kiran's Maternal Uncle And Udayvir's Brother in-law |
| Veena Singh | Ajay Singh's Wife |

# About the author

DEVI RAGHUVANSHI was born in Mathura, INDIA, the birth place of Lord Krishna and completed his Engineering Degree (B.E.) in Electrical Engineering. After working with big Corporates for 40 years, he ventured on a writing career.

This is his Twentieth book, in-depth peep through the Supreme sacrifice of a sister for her infertile sister, his first book "LOVE ON VENTILATOR", second book "LOVE TRIOLOGY, WHO TO COMPLAIN" , third book "IT'S OK TO FALL IN LOVE AGAIN" , fourth book "THE SON ROSE FROM THE WEST" , fifth book "MOHINI THE TIGRESS", sixth book "LOVE LOST IN TRANSIT" , seventh book "INDU THE PARCHED WOMAN", eighth book "MOTHER VS SURROGATE (A TALE OF TWO MOTHERS)", ninth book "IS THAT LOVE OR FANTASY?", tenth book "LOVE WILL THAT CHERISH OR

PERISH?", eleventh book "RUKHSAAR, THE WOMAN OF SUBSTANCE", twelfth book "URMILA-UNSPOKEN & UNAPPRECIATED", thirteenth book "RAGHU, THE SELF MADE MAN", fourteenth book "YE HOSLA KAISE RUKE" , fifteenth book "VIDUR (Archer, Strategist & Mahatma)", Sixteenth book "LOVE FROM THE OTHER WORLD", Seventeenth book "THE FLAME THAT STILL BURNS (NECROGAMY)", Eighteenth book "SHRUTIKIRTI (SITA'S SISTER)" and Nineteenth book "SHRUTIKIRTI (SITA'S SISTER)" – HINDI VERSION have already been published.

DEVI RAGHUVANSHI lives in MUMBAI and he follows Sports as he himself has been a state level athlete.

He can be followed on www.facebook.com/ds.raghuvanshi.9 or https://linktr.ee/AuthorDeviRaghuvanshi or Twitter @ Raghuvanshi_DS

# Author more books

**1st - LOVE ON VENTILATOR**

Ajit never felt insulted as he understood the mental agony and turmoil of Sudha. He will never leave Sudha with a broken heart and hope. He was not to satisfy his adrenaline rush as he had a firm belief that desire as a reason for mating is the way of animals.

**2nd - LOVE TRIOLOGY WHO TO COMPLAIN**

She was not responding to people and surrounding activities. The doctor arrived and after examination termed this as COMA or COMATOSE. He advised Ajit to treat it as medical emergency.

**3rd - IT'S OK TO FALL IN LOVE AGAIN**

She also knew that a single woman, both at home, college or at work, has to face many advances from men young and old, married and unmarried.

To be single and specially an unwed mother is taken as that she is available or easy to gain access to.

## 4th – THE SON ROSE FROM THE WEST

Anandita told Anwar – You are a Muslim completely different than what I preach and practice. I understand that your laws on marriage are different than ours so our alliance and resonance will need to be defined by you well before, we take a plunge.

## 5th – MOHINI THE TIGRESS

Mohini was considered as second degree manslaughter but Kuldeep always knew that there had to be a reason for her action. She was not born criminal from her mother's womb. He would marry her no matter what the consequences would be.

## 6th – LOVE LOST IN TRANSIT

"Everyone has a right to live life on his or her terms so why not Sandra?" She thought to herself. Just because she was a divorcee it didn't mean that her sex life had to dry. Sandra was young and had her bodily needs so she was sometimes finding her life entering a second phase of her sexual life.

## 7th – INDU THE PARCHED WOMAN

Ajay was restless wondering how would he react when Pihu would touch him. The bedroom smell divine like rose petals were sprinkled everywhere. It was extremely romantic and fragrance of Pihu, ignited his senses. They could see the view of half city and full moon over the Arabian Sea.

## 8th – MOTHER VS SURROGATE (A TALE OF TWO MOTHERS)

Monika would never take initiative like any western or high profile girl to propose to Ravindra even if she liked him. She would want Ravindra to do something crazy to win her over though she always loved a bit fantasy of being chased.

## 9th – IS THAT LOVE OR FANTASY?

Afreen was like a child, innocent but bonded with big dark eyes under some sort of fear. Sometimes in those moments in the dining room, Manzoor would prelong conversation which implied that he wanted to sleep with Afreen. Afreen usually used to get nervous but a mental strength was developed beneath Afreen's physical fragility. She used to leave him, got food for herself and went to other room bolted it from inside as she was always scared because she was a tiny sophisticated female and Manzoor this big tall guy.

## 10th – LOVE WILL THAT CHERISH OR PERISH?

Her brain was still deep in mourning but other parts of Amy were in overdrive reminding her that she was still alive, healthy and up for fun. Casually when Amy discussed this state of her mind and body to one of her very close friend of college era, she suggested this to be normal and good for her in getting back on the horse. The same friend also commented that our sexuality is a gift of God to be proud of. "She agreed that despite being raised conservatively by a father on the Church, we cannot challenge the physical design of God."

## 11th – RUKHSAAR, THE WOMAN OF SUBSTANCE

Frankly speaking I have not come to rebuild my relationship but just to remove the guilt from my mind and soul for I have hurt you and your family. I can't live with this guilt my life time. This guilt is becoming unrelenting source of pain and this kind of guilt is insidious and self-destructive.

## 12th–URMILA-UNSPOKEN&UNAPPRECIATED

One day, I will walk alone to the Sharyu. I shall light a pyre all by myself. When Sita wanted a pyre, you made it for her, but in my case, I will have to do it myself. I will do that. Sita entered the pyre to prove her purity, but I don't have to prove anything to anybody. I will not come out of the fire unscathed. I just want to annihilate myself. That night will be my last night of loneliness, rejection, abandonment and longing.

**13th – RAGHU, THE SELF MADE MAN**

During summers, we used to sleep in open sky area. One day I did notice that I was covered by the bed sheet to avoid cold and dew and it was done by the eldest daughter. Afterwards it became my habit of not covering myself with the hope that it will be done by her. It was actually done so long as I continued sleeping in the open.

**14th – YE HOSLA KAISE RUKE**

Life won't stop for you. Life can not stop for anyone. If it did we would never get anywhere. Instead of grieving and loving one man (Abhimanyu), Love the whole world.

**15th – VIDUR (Archer, Strategist & Mahatma)**

Vidur was an archer better than Arjun. He was a strategist for both Dhritarashtra and Yudhistar. He was the biggest devotee of Lord Krishna. He died as Mahatma. His Rajdharma did not allow him to fight. His Vidur Neeti is a guiding force even today.

## 16th – LOVE FROM THE OTHER WORLD

Abhimanyu was an army brat. After his engineering graduation he joined Google. He married Divya Singh, his IITD college mate. They had a son Parikshit. During Abhimanyu's vacations he went for mountain expedition at Mountain Kamet but never returned. Divya upon insistence of her parents and in-laws married her colleague Ranveer Singh. What happens hereafter…

## 17th – THE FLAME THAT STILL BURNS (NECROGAMY)

He told Captain Abhimanyu Singh and Anandita Singh to marry Mahi, the dead daughter of them. It was weird, socially, legally to think about marrying a dead body of our daughter Mahi and for an army officer it is next to impossible to let it happen but Ravi was polite but adamant.

## 18th – SHRUTIKIRTI (SITA'S SISTER)

Shrutikirti was daughter of King Kushadhwaj, King Janak's younger brother and queen Chandrabhaga. When Ram, Sita and Laxman were away in forest, Bharat and Mandavi in Nandigram as hermits, Urmila in deep sleep, it was Shrutikirti who managed the affairs of Kingdom along with her husband. She protested against Ram for asking Sita's fire test.

## 19th – SHRUTIKIRTI (SITA'S SISTER) – HINDI VERSION